P9-CZV-766

# DRAGON'S BAIT . . .

"Nidhoggr," I whispered.

No answer.

I began to climb the mountain of gold. And then he noticed me. The vast head rose high, high above me. A stray five gallons of dragon's napalm dribbled between his teeth and melted its way into the gold.

"Human," the dragon said. "I do not see my stone, my spear, my sword, or my cauldron."

"No," I said, speaking as loudly as I could.

"You are not looking well."

"No."

"You have mere hours left, human. The stone in your chest is impatient to burn you."

I nodded. "Yeah. I know all that. I also know how you can get your stuff back."

The huge eye before me widened in surprise.

"The fairies want your treasure. The Hetwan want to invade the Underworld, and they don't want to have to fight you to do it."

Nidhoggr nodded very slightly, like seeing the Goodyear blimp bob up and down. "The Hetwan. Ka Anor. He has designs on Hel."

"That's the plan. I think the Hetwan helped the fairies construct a weapon to kill you if you showed up over Fairy Land."

"Tell me about this weapon," Nidhoggr rumbled.

"No. Not until we make a deal. . . ."

Look for other EVERWORLD titles

by K.A. Applegate:

*#1 Search for Senna*
*#2 Land of Loss*
*#3 Enter the Enchanted*
*#4 Realm of the Reaper*

# EVER WORLD

## DISCOVER THE DESTROYER

K. A. APPLEGATE

SCHOLASTIC INC.
New York Toronto London Auckland Sydney
Mexico City New Delhi Hong Kong

ISBN 0-590-87762-3



12 11 10 9 8 7 6 5 4 3 2 1 0 1 2 3 4 5 6/0

Printed in the U.S.A.

First Scholastic printing, January 2000

For Michael
and Jake

# Discover the Destroyer

# Chapter I

They had taken my sword from me. Galahad's sword. My sword. Mine.

Christopher and Jalil and April, they'd told me to give it up, hand it to April. Why? Because of Senna. Because they couldn't trust me, so they said, couldn't count on me as long as she was around.

How many times had I come through for them, for us all? How many times had I stood out front, not alone maybe but out on the line, out at the point where danger pressed closest?

How many times had I been ready to give my life, to do what I had to do, and this? To be casually pushed aside with a smirk and a leer?

David can't handle Senna. David wants it too bad, man. David is hers, all hers to control, Senna's boy, Senna's pawn.

Under her spell.

I was. I knew that, and knowing that, I could fight her, resist her, even when she reached for me and touched me and I felt the power that flowed from her, the power that was sometimes so cold and demanding and sometimes so warm, so right, so . . .

I resisted her. Yes, yes, she had power. Yes, she could reach me. But I was a free man, free to say yes or no, free to make the calls as I saw them.

She was beautiful, Senna was, but it was more than that. In the real world I'd have had a dozen names for it, more excuses than explanations really. I'd have said she was seductive, that she fascinated me, that we had some certain chemistry.

But here, in Everworld, in this universe where the rules were all different, where nothing was what it had always been and yet was so often what it should be, here I knew the name for her power.

Magic.

She had magic. Senna the witch had power, and yet I was a free man. I was still David Levin. Senna could not change that.

And now, now with death looking down at us, death so clear and unmistakable and irresistible, now my friends gave me back the sword.

I had it back. When Nidhoggr had raised his ten-times-Tyrannosaurus head up from the mountain of gold, April had handed it back without a word.

I held it now. Held the hilt that would burn some men's hands, held it tight, the blade down at an angle, pointing down toward more wealth than I could imagine.

I had tried to kill a dragon once and failed. Failed so completely that the dragon had barely noticed my presence.

The dragon that I could not kill might have been Nidhoggr's puppy.

The idea of attacking this blue-whale-sized, diamond-armored monster was a sick joke. I was a mosquito and Galahad's sword was my stinger. If Nidhoggr had chosen to lie there passively, immobile, allowing me all the time I needed, I might, might in a long day of backbreaking effort have managed to hack my way into one of his vital organs. If Nidhoggr were in a coma I might have managed to kill him. But alive, alert? No.

And yet, I had the sword again. And with the sword came the responsibility, the unspoken demand to "do something."

Here you go, David, we're screwed now, so be the hero again. You die first.

It made me mad. Resentful. Now, when there

was not a single damned thing I or anyone else could do, now when the sword was as much use as a salad fork, now, suddenly, it was mine again.

Do something, David. We trust you again. Here: Take the sword and go kick Godzilla's butt.

But my resentment was tempered by several facts. First, the overwhelming fact that our lives were entirely in the claws of Nidhoggr. Second, the fact that we were standing atop a pile of treasure so vast that to count it I'd have to figure out what number came after "gazillion."

We were going to be sacrificed on an altar worth more than many major countries. And the strangeness of that, coming as it did directly on the heels of our escape from the half-living, half-dead, all-dangerous Hel and her charming brother the Midgard Serpent, took some of the steam out of my purely personal resentments.

Nidhoggr had been robbed. Four items had been taken from his treasure. A stone, a spear, a sword, and a cauldron were missing. They were special. Magic. And yet a part of me, some echo of my old-fashioned, ranting socialist grandfather was outraged. I mean, how much treasure did any one dragon need?

We stood there, the five of us, on a three-story, block-long mesa, a plateau of gold, diamonds, emeralds, rubies, crowns, scepters, armor, swords, and assorted fantastic bric-a-brac. We stood there — five dumb kids from north of Chicago — and stared up at a dragon so big he could have eaten Wrigley Field in about as many bites as it'd take me to eat a hot dog and actually heard him cry in rage as he denounced the leprechauns.

Leprechauns had stolen his stuff and run off to Fairy Land.

And that's when I volunteered to get his stuff back for him. The alternatives weren't good: Nidhoggr could eat us, or Nidhoggr could incinerate us. Or we could cut a deal.

"What the hell are you talking about?" Christopher demanded of me. "Leprechauns? We're going to go get this guy's magic soup bowl back from the leprechauns? What are you, nuts? We can't just take a rest somewhere?"

I looked at Christopher. Waited till he returned my stare. "Christopher, leprechauns are *very* little. This dragon is *very* big."

Christopher blinked. "You make a good point," he said.

"I . . . I thought leprechauns made shoes," April said.

"Old World nonsense," Nidhoggr rumbled in a low mutter that nearly made my ears bleed. "In the old times all the fairies were under control. The druids checked them. The Fianna limited their power. And of course the great gods themselves held their mischief in check. Oh, in the old times none of the fairy folk would have dared to steal from Nidhoggr! The Daghdha would not have allowed it! Times have changed. These fairies today . . ."

"The Daghdha?" April repeated and looked at Jalil, who shrugged. "Who is the Daghdha?"

"The great father god of the Celts, ignorant blasphemers!" the dragon yelled with a blast of wind that would have blown a sailboat halfway to Maui.

"So where is he, the Daghdha? Maybe he could get your treasure back."

Nidhoggr seemed just the slightest bit embarrassed by the question. The man-high iris of his nearest eye narrowed a few degrees. "The stolen goods belonged to the Daghdha. They . . . came to me, after the Daghdha was eaten by Ka Anor."

"Uh-huh," Christopher said. "That clears it all up for me. Let's get going, hi-ho hi-ho, it's off to Fairy Land we go. No problem. We'll get your stuff."

"Nidhoggr is not a fool," the dragon said. "You say you will bring me back what is rightfully mine. But I require something more binding than your word alone."

"I could leave you my backpack," April suggested.

Nidhoggr smiled and showed teeth silhouetted by the red magma, the burning napalm inside his throat. "I have a better idea."

Suddenly, from the ground before us, up from the mass of gold, rose four figures. Like trolls, thick-limbed, thick-armed, but smaller. Or did they just look smaller with Nidhoggr as a big-screen backdrop?

Each held in his rough, three-fingered paws a ruby, glittering, bloodred. Each ruby was the size of a fist. Larger. The size of a human heart.

The trolls held them out so that the rubies lay in their palms, like offerings.

"You're going to pay us?" Jalil wondered.

Nidhoggr laughed. The noise of his laughter became a physical force that sucked the air out of my lungs.

And then, as we watched with horrified fascination, the four rubies began to beat. Beat. Beat.

And inside my chest I felt a sudden stillness. A quiet, an absence no man has ever felt and lived to tell of.

My heart, my living, beating heart was in the hands of Nidhoggr's troll. The ruby was in my chest.

"The stones will give you life for six days," Nidhoggr said. "Return in six days with my treasure, and you may take your hearts again."

"Six days, we don't have any way, I mean, what, what if it takes longer than that?" April demanded. She was pressing her hand against her chest, searching, not finding.

"In six days the rubies in your chests will burn with Nidhoggr's own fire. Serve me well, and live. Fail me, and die."

Four rubies exchanged for four hearts. Only Senna stood unchanged. I wondered why. I knew the answer would terrify me.

"Go. Bring what is mine."

# Chapter II

"Well, here's kind of an obvious question: Why doesn't Large and Crusty back there go get his own damned stuff?" Christopher demanded. "I mean who is going to argue with him? King Kong vs. Nidhoggr comes up with The Crust doing the victory boogie twenty seconds into round one. And he can't handle some bunch of leprechauns?"

It was a good question. I said so. Which encouraged Christopher.

"Here's another good question: Just how are we supposed to find Fairy Land or whatever?"

"Yep, that's two good questions," I said. "But right now maybe we need to focus on putting a lot of distance between us and Nidhoggr, the Midgard Serpent, and Hel."

We had a mission. I was in charge. Not trusted,

not as long as Senna walked silently beside me, but in charge.

"That's another thing: Isn't anyone around here named Joe? Or Steve?"

We were walking along a tunnel. We were heading steeply uphill and had been for more than an hour, but I still didn't have the sense we were near the surface. Let alone what surface we might be near.

There was a stone, a ruby inside my chest. Right where my heart should be. And in six days it would burst into flame and kill me. We were thirsty, hungry, exhausted. Our heads, or at least my head, was full of recent memories of unspeakable horror.

But I was feeling strangely upbeat.

At last a straightforward job. At last a goal, a compelling need, a unifying, simplifying ambition. We had to get Nidhoggr's treasure back to him or else die. In six days. And I was pretty sure the ancient dragon wouldn't be giving extensions.

"He's too big," Jalil said. "He's been down in that hole, down at the bottom of that volcano shaft or whatever it is, and he's been growing bigger over the years."

"So what?" Christopher said.

"So that's why he can't go after the leprechauns himself," Jalil said.

"He's got wings, man. He could fly straight up. Up and out."

"I would say that's impossible," Jalil said. "But I've learned my lesson about what's possible and not possible here. Still, he must not be able to go after the leprechauns or else he'd go, not send us. And the leprechauns must have known he couldn't chase them or else what leprechaun in his right mind would rip him off? And how far gone am I that I'm even talking about the state of mind of a leprechaun?"

I was waiting. Waiting for Christopher to ask the next question. The third obvious question. But it was April who did it.

"Five of us. Four rubies for four hearts," she said. She looked at her half sister, but Senna kept her eyes straight ahead.

Christopher jumped right in. "Oh, come on, April. You know Senna's got no heart."

Senna said nothing. Her face revealed nothing.

"Um, Senna? Hey. Hey, you, witch lady?" Christopher was prodding her, trying to get a rise out of her. And out of me, too. Looking for an excuse to demand that I give up the sword. Looking for evidence that I was Senna's puppet.

"I say, witchy woman? Do you have a heart? I'm just curious. I mean, it's like a medical question, really."

Silence. Indifference. Senna's mind was off somewhere far away. She had her own take. She had her own motives. Maybe she saw deeper into things. Or maybe she just focused on her own agenda.

I would think I had her. I would think I understood. I would think, again and again that there was something real between us. But I'm not blind, not a complete fool. I wanted her. She wanted to use me. That's a big gap. I meant the same to her as a hammer means to a carpenter.

Change the subject. "Jalil, you've been keeping notes and drawing maps and all. Do you have any idea where this tunnel may come out?"

Jalil barked a laugh. "It could come out in Loki's dungeons for all I know. Or in Fenrir's butt. You can't make a map of what has no logical organization. It's a twenty-four-hour boat ride from frozen Viking country to steamy Aztec land. Then it's a brief walk to what could easily be the English countryside. And a few days' walk to Hel, where we fall down a very deep hole and land with only minor bruises, and you wonder if I have a map?"

"Spock, we're counting on you, Spock!" Christopher mocked.

After that we walked in silence for a while. Christopher seemed burned out. He falls into these funks for a while where he finally shuts up. But that's normal enough.

It was April who had me worried. I don't know what it is between April and Senna, but whatever it is, it's bad. Jalil and Senna dislike each other. Christopher treats Senna with the same contempt-masked-as-humor as he does the rest of us. But April hates Senna. Hates. And hate isn't an emotion that comes lightly or easily to April.

They share a father, April and Senna. Dad had an affair, I guess, with Senna's mom. Then Mom took off, and her dad stepped up and took responsibility for raising Senna. He brought her into his home.

Senna and April became instant sisters. Maybe that's all there is to it. Maybe it's just some kind of sibling rivalry thing. I'm no shrink; that's not what I'm good at. People's motivations, all their deep, dark stuff, I don't get. Not usually, anyway. Or else I get it a week later than everyone else.

"I think I see stars," April said. "Up ahead."

I peered ahead. The tunnel had a sort of background light, faintly reddish. Of course it made no sense. The light just seemed to glow. Why? Because it did. That's my answer for the mysteries of Everworld. Why? Because. Move on.

Jalil was the one who obsessed over the why and the how. Maybe he'd write the guidebook to Everworld some day: Galahad's castle definitely worth a stop. But avoid Hel's Underworld Club Med.

I squinted, shutting out as much of the background light as I could. Stars? Maybe. I inhaled deeply. A smell, yes, was it flowers? Maybe perfume. April, maybe.

No, that was dumb. April had had as little shower and soap time as the rest of us.

"I smell flowers."

"I smell you," Christopher grumbled. "I see the stars, though. It's night. Must be. How is that? Wasn't it daylight back when we were looking up from Large and Crusty's gold pile?"

"W.T.E.," Jalil said.

Welcome To Everworld. The shorthand answer to all of Everworld's bizarreness.

Definitely night sky ahead at the end of the tunnel. Definite stars. And now a slice of moon. I almost cried. The moon. The sky. After so long underground.

"Hello, up there," I said quietly. "Wasn't sure I'd ever see you again."

April breathed a huge sigh of relief. "I don't know if I mentioned this, but I have not been having a good time down here. Let's go before it turns out to be some sick trick."

Tired as we were, we quickened our pace. April shouldered her backpack, I hitched up my sword. Even Senna moved faster.

It was no trick. I saw the moon now peeking in and out between tree branches. Stars winked. The air was heavy with a smell I identified from when I was a kid and would visit my grandfather's place on Maryland's eastern shore. Honeysuckle. Normally I'd just say "flower," but this was one smell I actually knew by name.

The tunnel ended. I drew my sword and stepped out in front. Noticed that no one else volunteered for that job. Stepped out, sword at the ready, not really scared, not after what we'd come from. I didn't expect to ever see anything that would scare me as badly as Hel had.

I was standing under a night sky. Like the stars of home? I didn't know; I'm no astronomer. I was at the edge of a wood, trees not so tall as the forest we'd traveled to reach Hel's land. These trees seemed, even in the darkness, less gloomy. There was less of whatever unarticulated instinct would make my hair stand on end.

The ground above the cave entrance sloped gently up toward a low, tree-dotted hill.

I listened. Heard nothing but breeze in the trees. Maybe a suggestion of falling water, couldn't be sure. The point was, it wasn't Hel's underworld, it wasn't Nidhoggr's treasure room, it was open skies and blowing breezes and rustling leaves and the smell of sweet flowers.

I couldn't help it. My eyes filled with tears. Couldn't help it. Too much bad in my head. Too much fear-sweat dried on my skin. Too much adrenaline residue in my veins. Too many pictures, live-action, full-color, HDTV so real pictures in my memory. So many, how would I ever have room for anything else in there? What could ever claim a place between the scenes of horror?

I took a couple of deep breaths. Brushed the tears away. *Forget it all. Try to forget it. Act like you've forgotten it, David.*

"Come on out."

Jalil had already stepped out to stand beside me. "I wonder if the moon is real. Stars and all, too."

"Real enough, man."

"You know, way back, back in ancient times,

people believed the sky was this big upturned bowl. The sun traveled within it during the day. At night the light of the heavens came through little pinpricks in the bowl. That was stars. Little holes in an upside-down bowl."

"Yeah?"

"Yeah. And you know what's a bitch? Here that may actually be true." Then, in a very different voice he said, "If I knew how to do it, man, I would cut all that back there, everything we saw in the Underworld, I'd cut it out of my brain. I'd take a knife and cut it out of my brain. Damn, the moon is beautiful."

That's when we heard the scream.

"I didn't hear that," Christopher said, coming up behind me.

"Someone screamed," I said, momentarily not realizing that of course he'd heard it. "Sounded like a girl."

"Yeah, well, someone screams about every twelve seconds here, man, and it's usually me."

"Have to check it out," I said.

"No, you really don't," Christopher argued.

Senna spoke. I was surprised to hear her voice. She'd been silent for a long time. "It could be dangerous, David. And you have enough to deal with."

I felt the others holding their breath. Waiting to see. Would I snap to attention, say, "Yes, ma'am, Senna, sir!"

The scream came again. Closer. Definitely female. It sounded young. Panicked.

"You can all wait here," I said. "I'll be right back."

Ha. That would put them all in a dilemma. They wanted me to disregard Senna. But this time they agreed with her. At least Christopher and Jalil did.

"I'll go with you," April said.

We started down the last of the hill, down toward the no-longer-totally-benign woods. This was dumb, part of me knew that. But the day hadn't yet come when I could turn away from someone screaming for help.

I flashed on the men, the rows and rows of them, the thousands of them who right at this moment were buried up to their necks, their heads used as living cobblestones in Hel's monstrous world. They had cried for help, too. Were still crying for help.

We had walked across their heads, scuffed and scarred their tattered scalps, caught our heels in their hair. I hadn't rushed to save them.

I stopped. We were inside the first rows of trees. It smelled wonderful. Guilt stabbed at me. Those men. Those poor men.

*Save who you can, David,* I told myself. *Do what*

*you can. You couldn't kill Hel, couldn't change her, couldn't save her victims. Do what you can.*

*Be a man when you can,* I sneered. *Be a man when the odds aren't too long, when the risk isn't too great. Story of your life, isn't it, David?*

I heard pounding steps. Maybe hooves, but not horses, not that heavy. Maybe this wasn't so safe. Danger didn't always announce itself with quite Hel's flair for the dramatic or Nidhoggr's sheer power.

I heard a less mysterious sound. The others, joining me and April. I smiled to myself. *Can't trust me, and yet you can't avoid following me, can you? Well, that's okay. That's okay.*

"Aaaii!"

The scream was practically beside us. I whirled. Saw nothing. No, there had been something. A flitting trace of luminescent green.

And then, yes, hooves! The first one burst into view, flashes of furry, muscular haunches in uncertain moonlight. A horse? Small for a horse, short. Too small.

I gripped the sword. Friend or foe?

It was gone. Fast. Too fast, too agile to be a horse. It moved like a deer almost. And something was wrong with it, something that had left only a faint impression on my night-beguiled retinas. Something off.

Christopher whispered, "Can we not go ten minutes without some weirdness?"

A flash of green. So fast.

Then a bigger animal bursting from behind a tree, maybe a hundred feet away. Another coming in from the right. The two of them were vectoring in on the green light. And now a third. A scream came from the green creature, the blur.

Three against one. Not hard to guess what side I was on.

They were laughing. Laughing like drunken frat boys at a kegger.

The green thing shot toward us, stopped so suddenly you'd have thought the deceleration would leave her unconscious. And it was a definite she.

She stopped, wary, jumpy, almost vibrating with energy. She was between us, using us as a screen. Hiding behind us.

She was green. Not a little green, a lot green. I could see the color because she glowed like a paper candle lantern. Like she was filled with neon gas. She glowed the green of a spring leaf. Her skin, her face. Her hair was a darker green, like the same leaf in late summer. Her eyes, I didn't see them at first, couldn't because they darted this way and that, but when they paused for a microsecond they were yellow. Sunflower yellow.

She wasn't naked. But what she wore was a purely symbolic cover. She was no more than four feet tall. But a definite young woman, not a girl.

With a thunder of hooves and a spray of sweat, two creatures skidded to a halt in front of us.

"What the . . ."

They were a little smaller than me, the height of a short man. And if you looked only at the muscular, slightly pigeon-chested torso, they were men. Men with arms too slender for their chests, with narrow shoulders. Their chest, their shoulders were hairy. Not animal hairy but Sean Connery hairy.

Their heads were something other than strictly human, although in overall shape they might have belonged to men. But the ears were pointed, elongated, and furry. Their hair started low down on their brow, leaving barely an inch between hairline and eyebrows.

The eyes were without whites. The mouths were filled with large, flat teeth, like someone had moved all their molars to the front. They wore beards, wispy on the sides, more luxuriant coming right off the chin.

And none of that was the strange thing about them. The strange thing was that from the waist down they had the bodies, the tails, the hind legs of animals. Deer? Horse? No, not quite. No, more like goats. Like large goats. One the color of putty, one almost black.

Centaurs? I searched for the right word. No, centaurs were supposed to be half horse. And they'd have had four legs. These things ran on two hooved hind legs.

"Jalil?" I whispered.

"Got me, man," he said, shaking his head.

"Satyrs," April said. "Like in *Midsummer Night's Dream.*"

"Saturns? Like the cars?"

"Satyrs. Y-R-S."

The satyrs grinned. One of them hefted a wine-skin and shot a perfect stream of red wine into his upraised mouth. Both satyrs staggered a bit. Maybe just a result of balancing their ungainly bodies on two hooves. More likely a result of the wine.

"Step aside, mortals, and let us claim our delectable prize, ha-ha!" the third satyr said, slurring like a sophomore trying to convince his parents he wasn't faced. The one who had come silently up behind us. "The nymph is ours, be so kind as to stand aside. Although when we are done . . . and we shall surely finish eventually ah-hah-hah-hah . . . you can have her in trade for this bright, red-haired wench of yours."

The putty-colored creature in front of us leered at April, winked, and made a hip-pumping gesture.

"Wine!" his black-furred companion roared suddenly. He tilted back his head and waited while his compatriot squirted a stream of red wine toward his mouth. Putty missed several times and wine sprayed all over the black satyr's face.

"Now run away, mortals," the satyr behind me said. "Shoo! Shoo! The nymph is ours by right of conquest and you already have two lovelies of your own. Hurry off before we take them, too, ah-hah-hah. Ah, we'd make a night of it, eh? Eh, my brothers!"

"A night! A night!"

"Poems would be written, plays performed, ah-hah-hah, the romp of the satyrs! Come with me, lovelies, there's enough of me to satisfy all."

I turned around. This satyr was a little bigger. His fur was a sandy brown.

"I have a better idea: You guys walk away, leave the whatever, the nymph here, alone."

Sandy blinked. In his left hand he held a pottery jar. He raised it to his lips and took a long drink. He belched. Started to say something and belched again instead. Then he said, "We have chased this nymph all through the night. We are randy from the hunt! Ha-ha! We will not be denied, mortal. Be wary." He shook his finger side to side, laughing all the while. "You are not so unlovely yourself. I may be so drunk I'll not care whether I consort with nymph or mortal woman or mortal fool, ah-hah-hah-hah! Turn around, mortal, and let me see if you'll do in place of the nymph. Hah-hah-hah!"

Shouldn't bother me, it was just a dumb, drunken joke. Junior high stuff. Shouldn't make the adrenaline surge, shouldn't make my muscles tighten. Shouldn't. Did.

I waited till the three satyrs stopped laughing. Wait. Watch. Then I said, "I will stick this sword into your hearts."

Sandy blinked again. He took another drink. He peered closely at me. "Are you not from around these parts, then? Is that the problem? Do you not know that a satyr may claim any nymph he can catch?"

I glanced at the nymph. She was breathtakingly beautiful. Aside from being green. Her golden, bright eyes were fearful. And more than a little creepy.

"Do you want to go with these guys?" I asked.

"Of course she doesn't want to go with them," April exploded. "Does she want to be gang-raped in the woods? What kind of a question is that to even ask?"

I opened my mouth to say something in my own defense but couldn't think of anything to say. I closed my mouth. I was distracted. Memories deeper than those of Hel. Memories and dreams, and memories of dreams, had squeezed the rage into my veins, the sick physical need to lash out.

It wasn't about the nymph, not to me. It was about finding a moment, feeling the balance tip between restraint and attack. I just needed the excuse.

But April had her own needs, I guess. She stepped toward the boss satyr, the sandy-colored one. "We just escaped from Hel. You know Hel? Norse goddess of the Underworld? Well, we just came from her little amusement park, so if you drunken jerks think you're going to scare us, guess again."

The three satyrs looked at one another, shrugged, and seemed confused as to what to do or say next.

"Plus, this chick's a witch," Christopher said helpfully, jerking a thumb at Senna. "She can put the whim-wham on you dudes."

"Whim-wham?" the black satyr echoed.

Christopher nodded solemnly. "The whim-wham. The witch puts the whim-wham on you, well, how do I say this? You don't have any, shall we say, interest in nymphs anymore. None. Zero.

You end up not being satyrs anymore. You end up being, like, you know, like monks if you see what I'm getting at here."

Sandy stepped around to get a close look at Senna. Three sets of bleary, drunken satyr eyes peered solemnly at her.

"The whim-wham," Christopher intoned solemnly. "She did it to me. Ever since then I'll be running through the woods, nice and drunk, I'll spot a nymph, and you know what? I fall asleep, man."

Long silence. Dark looks at Senna. Pitying looks at Christopher.

"This nymph is as ugly as an old crone," Sandy said. "I would not stoop to consorting with her. Come, brothers, let us go and leave this nymph for others with less refined tastes."

The satyrs backed away cautiously till they were well back into the bushes, then turned and ran, almost as fast as the nymph herself had.

April laughed. "Not bad, Christopher."

He shrugged. "It's what you said once: These people believe any kind of b.s."

"David!" April yelled.

I turned, whipped the sword into a horizontal position, and caught the onrushing satyr about waist level.

Galahad's sword was sharp. Not as sharp as

Coo-Hatch steel, but sharp. The blade bit. My forward momentum met the satyr's opposite momentum. He was coming fast, too fast even to slow down.

The blade sliced clean through. I felt the impact, then the sudden release of drag as the blade cleared.

The top half of the satyr fell off, landed with a heavy plop on the ground. The bottom half kept running.

No sprays of blood. No cries of pain.

The nymph squealed, but whether it was delight or horror I couldn't tell.

"You cut off my legs!" the sandy-colored satyr cried in outrage.

"More than your legs," one of his companions remarked. "You're chopped in half. There goes your satyrhood!"

"Stop gaping, go get my legs!"

My first stunned thought was that the satyr was just taking a while to die. But the two uninjured satyrs were more puzzled than alarmed. And meanwhile the lower half of Sandy kept running. It slammed into a tree, fell down, and had some difficulty getting back up. No hands.

When it fell I could see its insides. Even in the dim light I could see that they were wrong. No blood. No spilled intestines. There was a concavity that must have been a bisected stomach. But none of the messy goo of human organs.

It was as if the satyr were a mere sketch. Like no one had filled in the details. A diagram used to show the protective effects of Pepcid AC.

The two whole satyrs chased Sandy's lower half, all the while keeping a cautious eye on me.

"All I wanted was a good time, a revel!" Sandy moaned. "How will I revel now with my better half gone?"

Horrifying. But I was fighting the urge to gloat. You want to do me, bitch? Look at you now.

I looked at the satyr and wiped my sword on my pants leg. He didn't see. I was irrelevant to him. He didn't care. I sheathed the sword.

# Chapter V

"Let's go," I said.

I had to grab Jalil's shoulder to shake him out of his fascination stall.

We started walking, looking back frequently to watch the Three Stooges moments as the satyrs tried to marry up the running lower half with the complaining top half of their leader.

The last we heard of them was Sandy calling for a fresh bottle, then crying pitifully that the wine was running straight out of him.

I looked at the nymph, then looked away, feeling embarrassed. She was fascinating. Like meeting an alien or something. But it really wasn't possible to look at her without staring.

Christopher had no such qualms. He stared openly, with an expression of curiosity, incredulity, and frank appreciation. April tried to offer her a supporting arm but the nymph seemed not to notice.

"You're free to go, miss," I said. I sounded like a cop releasing a suspect.

"Those satyrs could come at us again," Jalil pointed out. He was managing to stare everywhere but at the little green woman.

"Yeah, she needs to hang with us for a while, at least," Christopher said. He tried and failed to suppress a smirk.

April sighed, expelling the air through gritted teeth. It was a sigh loaded with harsh commentary on the three of us.

"Do you have a name?" April asked the nymph. "Can you tell us your name?"

No answer.

"Ask her if she has any sisters. I'd like the whole set: blue, red, purple. A nymph six-pack. Do they come in orange?"

"Christopher, shut up," April snapped. "She's lost and scared and alone, or aren't any of you capable of caring about that?"

April bent over, bringing her face level with the nymph's weird and lovely eyes. "Can you tell me your name?"

"I am called Idalia."

She had an amazing voice. Or maybe it wasn't the voice but the way she used it. Like she was singing the words. Not that there was a melody, there wasn't, but like she was singing anyway.

I realized I was smiling. Everyone was smiling. Even Senna showed some faint curving of her lips.

"You're a nymph, huh?" I said.

She blinked her eyes at me.

"What else would she be? The satyrs said she was a nymph." April had decided she was the nymph's spokeswoman and protector. Probably a good idea.

"What is the definition of a nymph?" Jalil wondered.

Christopher laughed. "Oh, I'd say green, about four feet tall, and built like —"

"Okay, that's it," April snapped.

"Oh, get over it, April," Christopher shot back. "It's not like we're going to put the moves on her; she's four feet tall. I mean, yeah, she looks like she's twenty-one but she's the size of a kid. Jeez, what do you think I am? I can't make a harmless joke? She's older than we are."

The nymph giggled. It was a sound like a stream chuckling over loose rocks. That's not a metaphor. That was the actual sound. "Good sir, friend mortal, I have lived as long as Everworld and longer still. I served the goddess Iris. And would still. But that is a tale for another time."

Christopher nodded. "Okay, she's over a thousand years old, which as far as I'm concerned means she can probably take a joke. And buy beer."

"Well, glad to meet you, Idalia," I said. That didn't sound right so I added, "Ma'am."

"You are well met, indeed," Idalia said.

"Will you be okay if we leave you here? I mean, do you think those satyrs are gone?"

"The satyrs are surely gone. They have long since forgotten about me and will return to drunkenly chasing shadows."

"Cool. Then I guess we'll see you around. We have a mission, sort of."

"A quest?"

"Absolutely. A quest. We have to find Fairy Land."

"And don't mention San Francisco," Christopher said.

"Christopher, do you just look for ways to be offensive?" April demanded.

Idalia cocked her head and peered curiously at me. It was absolutely as if she were made entirely of translucent green glass. Like looking at the sun through a spring leaf. You almost felt you should be able to see her insides, but you couldn't, of course. Maybe like the satyrs she didn't really have insides.

"Do you know the way to Fairy Land?" she asked.

Jalil answered for all of us. "Oddly enough, no. We'd be grateful for any help you can give us."

"We were going to ask at the next gas station." Christopher.

The nymph clapped her hands. "Then I will show you."

"You don't have to do that," Jalil said.

The nymph smiled at me. It was a thousand-year-old smile. It was a smile women had been making for a lot longer than that. Then her smile wavered. She glanced at Senna. Nervous, like she'd seen something she didn't like.

She moved suddenly. A green blur and she was before Jalil. Smiling at him. Jalil smiled back. Caught himself. Met her gaze again and smiled again.

Jalil is tall. Idalia is short. She comes up almost to my shoulder. On Jalil she reached his chest. Jalil was sort of bending over, bending his knees, slumping in a way he no doubt thought was subtle, bringing himself down to her level.

"I can show you the way to Fairy Land," she said to Jalil.

"We need a guide," Jalil said. He looked at me and scowled. "Well, we do."

"Uh-huh," April said skeptically.

Idalia put her tiny hand on Jalil's chest. "In gratitude for your heroism in saving me, I will be . . ."

She fell silent. The seductive, playful smile was gone. "Where is your heart?"

Jalil seemed stumped. Then he snapped, realized what she was saying. "Oh. Nidhoggr, this big dragon. He has it."

Idalia nodded, showing no more surprise or skepticism than if Jalil had told her his car was in the shop. Then she smiled again, tilted her head back to gaze up at Jalil with a politician's wife's adoring gaze. "When you have your heart again, maybe you will let Idalia borrow it? At least . . . for a night?"

Christopher laughed out loud. "Yeah, April, she's lost and scared and alone. You want to protect someone, take care of poor Jalil."

# Chapter VI

"Do you know the way to Fairy Land?" Christopher sang.

"Christopher, you have more useless old crap stuffed in your brain," Jalil complained. "What is that, like, some Glen Campbell? Some John Denver?"

"I don't even know," Christopher admitted. "Do you know the way to Fairy Land? La la lala la la lala la. I think I may have heard the Muppets singing it. How about, 'It's not that easy being green?' Idalia. Do you know Kermit?"

We were walking along under a gradually lightening sky. It was an easy walk. There wasn't a trail, but no trail was necessary. The trees were spaced just far enough apart to allow their outer branches to meet without entwining. There were few bushes, no thorns, no obstacles but an occasional stream requiring nothing more strenuous than a hop. And the *great* thing was, we now had water.

Finally we'd had enough to drink. We were still hungry but not faint, not weak from it. And we were putting miles between us and Hel, between us and the Midgard Serpent also known as Jormungand, and between us and Nidhoggr.

We were less than six days away from bursting into flames but even that fact seemed less than horrifying as we followed Idalia through countryside that only became more peaceful and unthreatening as the sun rose.

Of course, following Idalia wasn't quite what it sounded like. The nymph seemed incapable of moving at the cowlike pace of we humans. She would flit away, be gone for an hour, then come zipping back, a green blur, to stop, flirt with Jalil, make sure we were going the right way, and then disappear again.

"Idalia? Kermit? Kermit no-last-name. About, well, smaller than you, made out of a green towel and Ping-Pong balls for eyes? Does that ring a bell?"

Idalia flitted away.

"The Flash," Christopher said. "The girl is fast. Jalil, man, looks like you could get lucky there.

Could be the greatest two and a half seconds of your life."

I tried not to smile. Then I saw April smothering a laugh.

"Shut up, Christopher," Jalil muttered.

But of course Christopher had hold of Jalil now and wasn't going to let go. "I worry about your kids, you know? It's hard growing up torn between two cultures, not knowing if you're African-American or, you know, green."

"Too bad she doesn't seem attracted to you, Christopher," Jalil shot back. "Your kids would have had the perfect melding of her tiny body and your tiny brain."

"Oooh. Ouch! That hurts, Jalil, but I don't take it personally. I know you're just worried. Worried about that big moment: 'Mom, Dad, I'd like you to meet my girlfriend. Yes, Mom, she is green! Yes, Dad, I know she's only four feet tall! Why can't you two ever just be nice to my girlfriends? Why are you always so critical?'"

"David, I need to borrow the sword for a minute."

"Married life? A breeze. She'll clean house in under five seconds."

"You're such a sexist," April said. "What makes you think Idalia is going to be staying home and cleaning house? Maybe she'll have a job. Work outside the home."

"Maybe she can type. Maybe fifty, sixty thousand words per minute," Christopher suggested.

"Retail. She's a natural for Talbot's. Or any petites department."

"Now I'll need to borrow the sword for two minutes," Jalil said.

I said, "Tell you one thing: All joking aside, I'm glad to be dealing with people smaller than we are. Nymphs and leprechauns, that's gotta be better than big honking Lokis and Huitzilopoctlis and Fenrirs and Hels and Nidhoggrs."

"Don't be too certain of that," Senna said.

Once more I'd gotten used to the idea that she was silent. I'd almost managed to put her out of my mind.

"You have something to say, Senna?" Jalil asked in tense, measured tones.

"Do you know something about these fairies?" I asked her. "If you do, you need to let us all in on it."

For a few more steps she said nothing. Then, "Everworld is a dangerous place, David. How do little people, fairies and leprechauns, how do they survive here in a place filled with giant gods and giant monsters?"

I missed a step. Caught up. Noticed that

Christopher and April and Jalil had stopped their teasing.

"How do the weak ever stand up to the strong?" Senna asked.

I shrugged. "By, I don't know. By, I guess by standing together, staying united."

Senna didn't exactly roll her eyes. There was just a passing, cynical twist of her lips. "How many Idalias would have to unite to defeat one Hel? How many fairies to scare off Nidhoggr?"

"A lot," I admitted. "Too many. There couldn't be that many leprechauns."

I waited, we all waited, but Senna offered nothing more. Idalia flitted back, and left, and returned again. And as we walked through golden woods and across flower-strewn meadows, I wondered and worried.

Maybe Nidhoggr could fly. Maybe Nidhoggr could go after the leprechauns himself. Maybe Nidhoggr was scared.

What could possibly scare Nidhoggr?

That grim thought was pushed aside by a realization that I was hearing the sound of hooves. I spun, sword drawn.

Sandy's lower half ran by.

# Chapter VII

We made camp as the sun came up full and strong above a meadow of wildflowers. Was it the most beautiful place I'd ever been? Or was it so beautiful because it pushed aside memories of Hel's evil face?

Either way it was beautiful. And it felt safe. It was hard to imagine an evil that could exist in a place so full of tall, waving lavender and sprinkles of brilliant yellows and reds.

"We need some sleep," I said.

"I'm for that," Jalil agreed.

The bottom half of the satyr had crossed our path again. It slammed into a tree, fell down, then climbed up again.

"That's not too weird," Jalil said.

"I'll take first watch," I said.

We dropped where we were. Dropped down into the ankle-high grass in the shade of a small, isolated grove of peach trees beside a winding brook.

We yanked down as many peaches as we could easily reach. They were pink, ripe, sweet. Perfect.

"This place is a postcard," April said. "Organic peaches on top of everything."

"It's about time we caught some kind of break," Christopher said. "I mean, I'd still rather have a . . . fresh sheets . . . maybe a . . ."

He was asleep before he could finish the thought. Asleep with a bite of peach still caught in his teeth. I fought an urgent need to yawn. How long had it been since we'd slept? How long? Days? How could I even be sure when we'd been underground so long? It didn't matter anyway. We'd sleep here.

One by one they began to breathe more slowly, regularly. Some snored. Senna lay peacefully on her side, eyes closed. It was a relief to know that she did sleep. She was human, after all.

There was a beam of sunlight on her pale skin. She frowned and rolled over, leaving me only the back of her head.

I wanted to talk to her. Wanted to ask her so many things. Wanted to hear her answers. Or maybe just wanted to hear the answers I wanted to hear.

Long ago, back before all this had begun, or maybe not that long ago at all, anyway, back then I'd thought I was in love with Senna Wales. Back then she'd ridden in my car, talked with me, laughed with me. Kissed me. Lit a fire and sent it raging through me.

Back then she was a girl unlike any I'd met, different, but in a way I couldn't name or explain. Just different. Back then I'd wanted her. For what? For her legs, her breasts, her lips? For the way I never seemed to impress her, for the way she never minded that I was me? For the way she made me imagine a world that would be profoundly different because of her presence in my life? Why not?

Now all my feelings about her were suspect. Senna wasn't a girl anymore. She was an object wanted by so many, none of whom wanted her love. She was a secret. A danger. A power.

And she could make me want her, make me need her, make me believe her, buy my loyalty with that basic currency of Everworld: magic.

How was I supposed to know what was real now? How was I supposed to know my own truth when she could, with a touch, reach down inside me and twist me around?

Maybe it would have been a good thing to ask her all that. Maybe. But her back was to me, and Jalil and April and Christopher and a green creature out of a mythology book were all in the way.

We had little time to travel to a place we'd never been, recover Nidhoggr's loot, and get back to him with it. Maybe we could push the leprechauns around, get what we wanted. Maybe not.

We had a sword. A small knife. And a witch. I wondered, when the time came, whether Senna would be a weapon I could use.

"They have crossed into another world," Idalia said as she zipped back. She seemed surprised, perplexed.

"Yeah. That happens to us. We don't know why. For some reason whenever we fall asleep here we rejoin our lives in the real world. There's another me over there, too. Doing whatever I'd be doing. School, work, hanging out. When I go to sleep later I'll go there, too."

Where did Senna go when she slept? Did she cross back over into the real world?

The nymph laughed and her laughter woke Christopher just enough to cause him to spit out the peach. That was a relief. I would have had to pick it out of his mouth so he didn't choke.

"You call it the real world?" Idalia asked. "Is this not real as well?"

I shrugged. It was disturbing talking to Idalia. A little like going to a nude beach and trying to talk football with the first beach bunny you find. I wasn't attracted to Idalia. More like I was embarrassed.

"I guess Everworld is as real as our own world. But they all feel more like they belong over there."

"My Jalil, too?"

I noted the "my." Decided to let it go. Idalia was doing the smart thing: making sure that she had at least one of us on her side. She couldn't know whether to trust us. If she wanted to tease and enthrall Jalil, fine.

Part of me was resentfully glad to see it. Suddenly I wasn't the only one to be considered suspect for having a relationship.

I glanced at Senna's back. A relationship? Is that what I had with Senna? The word seemed ridiculous.

"Yeah," I answered belatedly. "I think Jalil feels more like the real . . . the Old World is his world."

"But not you?"

I shrugged. "I cope with what is. I try and deal with reality, you know, take it as it comes."

Again Idalia laughed. "Poor mortal."

And then she was gone in a green blur. So fast

that the grass had not sprung up from beneath her footsteps by the time she was out of my sight.

I breathed a sigh of relief. The nymph was an unknown. I didn't need unknowns right now. The known was enough trouble.

I pressed my palm down on my heart. No beat. Nothing. I took my pulse at my wrist. There the familiar rhythm still fluttered. Touched my neck. Blood still pumped through the arteries.

I touched my heart again. Nothing. Silence.

So weird. No man, no woman felt that absence and lived. So strange.

So . . .

I was in my car. Top up. It was raining. It was pouring, like someone was hitting my windshield with a fire hose. On the cracked, white leather seat beside me was the small paper bag that held the vacuum cleaner belt and two packs of bags. The radio was playing mostly static.

"No!"

I swerved. Caught myself. Avoided oncoming traffic. Sheridan Road was two lanes, oncoming traffic around every hairpin turn.

"Damn it," I cursed again and slammed the steering wheel with both hands. I had fallen asleep. I'd fallen asleep without waking anyone to take over my watch. We were lying there asleep, the five of us, without a guard.

Anything could simply walk up on us. Anything. And in Everworld the possibilities were endless.

Asleep on sentry duty. In a war they could execute you for that.

I felt the now-familiar disturbance as the two halves of me melded into a single me. Jalil had dubbed the experience "CNN — Breaking News."

That's what it was, a sudden flash of news as I, the me of the real world, the me driving the car and going to buy a vacuum belt for my mom, suddenly learned all that had happened to that other me. And vice versa.

It had been a long time since the last update. Memories burst unfiltered into my brain. Memories of Hel's face, her half-dead, maggot-eaten face, the squirming, abject terror. And the uncontrolled passion, need, desire whenever she turned her other face to us.

Images of men buried. Images of men lying in an eternal non-death beneath flagstones, buried alive, buried alive forever. Images of —

I yanked the car off the road. No room for it, not on Sheridan, so I ran the old Buick up some rich guy's driveway. I stopped. Gripped the wheel. Hands shaking. All of me shaking.

Had to throw up. I pushed the door, leaned out, just in time, just barely missed destroying my car. I vomited onto the driveway, rain pouring down on the back of my head, neck, shoulders. Rain diluting, washing away the mess.

I sat up. Used both hands to squeegee the water out of my hair. And there, holding a purple umbrella, was a woman. Middle-aged. Chunky, squat. Dark eyes in a hard face. Graying hair pulled back.

She was the maid from the big house at the end of the driveway. Had to be. People who lived in five-million-dollar lakefront mansions didn't dress like this or look like this.

"Sorry," I said.

"Come." She had an accent. What type I couldn't tell. With her free hand she indicated the house. "Come. Inside."

I shook my head. "I'm fine. Must be something I ate."

She stared at me, wouldn't look away, wouldn't release me. "You bring message."

"No, no, ma'am, you must be expecting someone else. I'm not the messenger. I just happened to be driving by and felt sick, and you know how the driving is on Sheridan, it's not like you can pull off onto the shoulder."

She moved closer. I wanted to close the door, the rain was running off the roof onto my carpet, and the carpet, what was left of it, didn't need any more mildew. But now she was blocking the door.

Suddenly she reached for me. She laid her hand over mine, warm and dry over the cold wet hand that rested on my partly raised window.

She maintained contact and what could I do? I'd just thrown up in her driveway, I wasn't in a position to tell her to leave me alone.

Her black eyes closed. Then opened wide, very wide. Surprise. Fear. But in the end her expression settled into concern. Maybe pity.

"The dark ones are close," she said.

I felt a chill creep up my spine. The dark ones. Nonsense. Coincidence. She was some superstitious old Mexican lady or Polish lady or whatever. Rich men's maids were all Mexican or Polish around here.

Coincidence. Then she said, "Has the gateway been opened?"

I froze.

"The what?"

"Must close," she said. "Must close gateway."

She turned and waddled back toward the house. The rain came down with renewed vigor and she disappeared from view.

I backed down the driveway. Through the gate.

I laughed in nervous relief. Gate. Gateway. Of

course. There was a gate and it was open. That's all she meant. The gate to the estate was open. Nothing to do with Senna.

"It's getting to you, man. You're starting to get freaked."

I was asleep over there, over in Everworld. I had fallen asleep and there was nothing I could do to wake myself — my other self — up. All I could do was go along through my day. Go through the usual motions like my head wasn't full of memories of a life I didn't really live.

All I could do was wait for the next update. That's all I could do, this me, real-world David. Wait and see what happened when the other guy woke up, lived out his day, and fell asleep again.

If he woke. If he lived.

I'd let everyone down. Failed. Fallen asleep on duty and now maybe everyone would die because of me. Would I ever even know? What would happen to me if the other David died? What would happen to him if I died? If I drove my car into an oncoming truck would Everworld

David die, or would Everworld David go on living and, when he fell asleep, simply dream dreams?

I drove home. Got soaked running into the house to give my mom the vacuum bags and belt. She made me put on the belt. I did it as fast as I could; I had to get out of there, had to get going. Nowhere to go but I had to go anyway. Had to find the others.

I called April. Not home. Called Jalil. Not home. It was a Saturday afternoon, big surprise, they were out. Called Christopher. His mom said he was grounded. He'd missed curfew the night before. Maybe I had something to do with it, she said, in which case maybe next time I was out late with him I should remind Christopher that he was to be home by midnight. Not ten after, not twelve-thirty, and definitely not one-fifteen A.M., by which time his father had been calling the hospitals looking for him.

I put on my solemn voice and assured her that no, I hadn't been with Christopher. Must have been some other friend of his. But could I talk to him for just a minute? I needed to know when the chemistry paper was due.

"Nice try," she said and hung up.

I drove to the Boston Market in Skokie. Jalil's car was parked in the lot. I found him working the counter in a mostly empty store.

"Those red potatoes are looking a little rank," I said.

"Then order the mashed," he said.

Jalil is not a person who is ever going to look happy wearing a name tag and an apron.

"You here for chicken?" he asked me.

I leaned in close across the counter. He backed away a few inches.

"I fell asleep, man."

"Uh-huh."

"I mean, I didn't wake anyone up to pull next shift. I fell asleep. We're all over there zoned out in the grass and no one watching out."

"What am I supposed to do about it?"

"Nothing, man, I'm just checking to see. I mean, maybe you woke up and pulled your shift, right? Maybe Christopher woke up on his own and then you pulled your shift after him."

"I don't think so."

The manager, a short, chubby, kind of hyper woman came over and bustled around in the display case. "Jalil, we need a new tray of reds."

"Told you they were getting skanky," I said.

"I'll take care of it," Jalil told his boss. "Listen, David, let's pretend this conversation never happened, okay? There's nothing you can do or I can do about over there. So in the meantime how about not letting Christopher and April know that you screwed up? You know? Your credibility isn't all that high right now."

That burned. "What do you mean? What are you talking about?"

"Don't play ignorant, David, you know what I'm talking about."

"Hey, you don't seem to mind having little what's-her-name, Idalia, pawing all over you."

"Red potatoes, don't forget," the manager called out in a chiding voice.

"Give it up, man. You think there's some analogy there?" Jalil said. "She's nice to look at. But that's it. All she's after is to pay her obligation to us for saving her and then to bail out and go do whatever it is nymphs do. She thinks maybe we'll go satyr on her; she wants to position me to control you and Christopher."

You had to admire Jalil's mind. There wasn't a lot of sentimentality getting in the way.

"I know Senna's using me," I said. "What's the difference? I'm handling Senna."

Jalil shook his head. "No one is handling Senna. You believe what you want, I know what I know. It's all about power for her, David. She sold us out to Hel because it suited her purpose. Right now it suits her to let us all get along. But that could change. When it does, well, we'll see, won't we?"

"Go get your potatoes," I snapped.

"I'm trying to help you out, man. I can separate out the fact that you're exhausted beyond belief so you go to sleep, I can separate that out from whatever else. Christopher? Not so sure he'd see it that way. He might get it into his head that this is all her doing. If it hits the fan again, and it will, we all need to know which way you'll jump."

"I'll do the right thing, you smug jerk, I'll do the right thing. You guys are quick enough to ask me what's what when there's some kind of danger."

Jalil nodded. "Yeah. You're right. But you know what, David? We're true-blue Americans, we're not some kind of Iraqis or Serbs or whatever. We're not in the Cult of David. None of us is into going down in flames. We don't do that whole 'follow the fool till he gets us all killed' thing." He grinned cynically. "You're our hero, David. Till you screw up."

I left. Got in my car and burned rubber on the way out of the parking lot. Burned rubber just like the dickweeds I can't stand.

I'd let Senna get to me. True. I'd fallen asleep. True. And there had been that whole first encounter with Loki. What had happened then was burned into my brain in blazing color.

I was messing up. I was failing. Ticktock till the ruby burned a hole in my chest and I was asleep and messing up and failing and what then? I felt the panic choke. Sucked in air.

I felt my chest. *Beat beat beat beat.*

I looked at my watch. I was due at work. Had to go on with life, that was the weird thing. I couldn't just throw it all away because in some different universe I was a different person. Still had to go to work, put in the hours, count out the grudging tips, save the paycheck for college expenses and a new starter for the Buick Beast.

I drove to Starbucks, parked, jumped out, slicked my wet hair back into some kind of order. Two of my fellow employees were having an end-of-shift smoke in the alleyway between Starbucks and the dry cleaners.

"T'sup, man?" one called to me.

"My life sucks," I muttered. "Both of them."

"Heard that."

I put in my four hours of dribbling espresso and steaming milk and trying to build a wall between me and memory, me and fear, me and the pressure of rush, rush, rush or fail. Asleep and no one trusted me. In love with a girl who had torn my life apart. Dribble another cup of espresso, steam up some more skim, and try not to think of the bitter and deserved recriminations if I failed.

After work I headed home. Real-world me was tired. Real-world me had stayed up late the night before trying to catch up on homework while watching the Bears lose in overtime.

I crawled into bed, clean, crisp sheets. Man, what a good feeling. Pillow. Blanket. Bottle of water on the nightstand.

I was asleep in two universes.

And awake in a third.

The cabin, oh, no, no, the cabin again.

Rows of kids sleep in wooden bunks, snoring beneath handmade banners proclaiming the superiority of our cabin over all the other cabins in the fields of canoeing and wood chopping.

The last fart jokes had all been enjoyed, the last teasing had died out, the good-natured threats of ass-whippings to be administered the next day had all been made.

The kids sleep. All but one.

The door opens, cool air, freshening air scented with sweat and paste and chocolate chips.

The white windbreaker. It's the windbreaker of the mighty, the counselors. It's Donny's windbreaker.

And the kids sleep, all but the one, all but the

one who squeezes his eyes shut and tries to fake it, thinking maybe that will work, maybe sleep will be a defense.

Defense? From what? He doesn't know. He doesn't have a word for it. It can't be named. Not part of his vocabulary, an experience without a word, a suffering without a name.

*Just yell, kid,* I say. *Just don't lay there and take it and pretend you're asleep, are you stupid? Are you a coward? Maybe you deserve it.*

I can't save him. I tell him, silently, I tell him what to do and I know he hears me, I know he hears me but he won't do it. Why won't he fight back? Why won't he resist?

My heart is pounding. I should do something. I should be brave. I should go to someone, tell someone, not cry silently with eyes squeezed shut, helpless.

Poor kid. Poor kid. I do nothing. Poor kid.

# Chapter X

The sun was afternoon strong, burning red through my closed eyelids. I blinked, shielded my face, and looked around. My heart was silent. Nothing moved in my chest.

The dream was gone. The dream of another me. But his dreams, his nightmares were mine, too, as my dangers were his. Memory shared all, made us both into one.

April asleep. Christopher asleep. Senna sitting, back to the rest of us, maybe asleep, maybe awake. Jalil was standing a few feet away. The nymph was with him. In the sunlight her skin seemed less translucent.

I got up. Sauntered as casually as I could over to the strange pair. Closer up I could see that Idalia's skin was covered with a leaf pattern. Like tiny interlocked oak leaves.

I stared. The effect was of a skintight leotard of leaves. It was at least a little bit more modest.

"It's the sun," Jalil explained. "She doesn't like the bright sunlight."

I might have made some remark about photosynthesis but this wasn't the moment. "So?" I said.

"So, after you woke me up for my shift I got confused, accidentally woke you up for the next shift and you got me back. You and I stood watch, just the two of us."

"That's the story?"

"That's the story."

I didn't have anything to say to that. Jalil was lying to protect my reputation. No, correction: He was lying because I was useful to him, to the group as a whole, and Jalil has a good, sharp eye for self-interest.

And for now that meant he owned me. A piece of me, at least.

"What do you want?" I asked him bluntly.

His eyes glittered, unreadable. Then he smiled. Flicked his chin with his fingertips and said, "The time may come when I will ask you to do a service for your Godfather."

I wasn't amused. Or fooled. Jalil might be presenting it as a joke but we both knew he meant it.

"Want to see something?" Jalil said. He pointed. "Down there. Through the gap in the trees."

I shaded my eyes from the glare and followed the direction he pointed. We were in a wide, poster-pretty meadow, with deciduous forest around us on three sides. The ground had a slight roll, just enough to raise the occasional patch of lavender or poppies or black-eyed Susans into view. But two rolls sort of met and formed a crease that went down through an open space in the trees. And down there, within easy view in the brilliant sunlight, was a wagon being pulled by two oxen. It was a massive, wooden-stake thing loaded with what looked like agricultural produce of some sort.

"Down!" I snapped and yanked at Jalil.

"Relax. It's been going on all morning, all afternoon. It's a road. Wagons, chariots, handcarts. They come along every few minutes. Going both ways. When it's not a wagon or whatever it's livestock: cows, pigs, a lot of sheep. Mostly going right to left."

I stood up again, cautious. Too late now to worry about being seen. "Same direction we're heading in."

"Idalia? What did you call that road?"

"It is called the Valley Road by some. The Fairy Road by others, or Oberon's Path. Some call it the Roman High Road."

"Why aren't we on that road?" I asked.

Idalia laughed. "I cannot walk there! It is not safe for my kind."

"Does it lead to Fairy Land or whatever? What is the name of this place we're going?"

"Yes, it leads to the Fairy Lands," Idalia confirmed.

"She can't leave the woods," Jalil said. "She's a wood nymph. We've been talking. She has to stay in the woods unless she's with her goddess, Iris. Greek goddess of something or other."

"Goddess of the rainbow," Idalia supplied.

"Yeah. Rainbow. Plus some kind of messenger."

"And why isn't she with this Iris?"

"She was banished."

"Yeah? Why?"

"You better tell him, Idalia," Jalil said. He looked away, affecting to be very interested in the half-a-satyr as it wandered aimlessly around through a field of brilliant yellow wildflowers.

"Oh, for loving a mortal."

I raised an eyebrow at Jalil. He refused to notice me.

"That's not approved of?"

Idalia laughed. "I approve of it. All nymphs approve, of course. There are no males of our own kind. Who should we love if not humans? Dwarfs are so ugly and anyway all they care for is work. Elves? Elf men are very beautiful but so are their women. They will not notice a nymph. And the fairy folk do not like my kind."

I nodded like all this made perfect sense. Nodded like this was all nothing new to me.

"It's very unfair," Idalia pouted. "We may not love a mortal but there is no one else to love. It is all very well for the great gods and goddesses, Zeus or Aphrodite or even that nasty old Hephaestus to take a human lover. Half-god mortals are everywhere to be found. What is Heracles if not the fruit of a mortal–immortal union?"

An answer seemed to be demanded. "I don't know."

"It's all well and good for the great gods to dally with a comely mortal but a nymph is never supposed to enjoy herself."

"So, what happened is you fell in love with a mortal so Iris basically fired you?"

Idalia nodded. "It is very unfair."

"Uh-huh. I can see where that'd be unfair, yeah."

"Each time I tell her that I am sorry, each time

I ask, 'What am I to do?' But every time she catches me, it's off to the forests until her wrath cools."

Jalil said, "And this has happened before? You being fired by Iris, I mean?"

Idalia laughed. "Oh yes. Hundreds of times. No matter how many mortals I hide from her, she eventually finds me with one."

"Explain this to David like you did to me," Jalil said. "You've been caught hundreds of times. But usually you don't get caught, right? So how many mortals have there been?"

Idalia laughed her babbling-brook laugh. "I don't count them all. Who could count them all? That would be so many. I would be spending all my time with my head crammed full of numbers."

"Makes you feel special, eh, Jalil?" I said.

He laughed. "It's what they do, man. I looked up nymphs after work, before I woke up. Nymphs. They come in all different types: dryads, hamadryads, naiads, nereids, oreads. They're a type of minor god. Beautiful young women attached to various big-league gods or else located in the woods, the ocean, so on. About all they do is fall in love with humans. 'Fall in love' being the discreet term they use. That and getting chased by satyrs."

"That's it?"

Jalil shook his head in disgust. "They're not evolved, see, they're created. Invented. Built by the gods, who I guess never really asked themselves what the nymphs were supposed to do beyond looking pretty and acting easy. They didn't evolve to fit into some ecosystem. They're basically interior decoration: like paintings the gods might hang around Olympus to make the place look good."

"W.T.E.," I said.

"That corner looks a little bare. I know, let's get two or three nymphs. Green, I think, to go with the couch."

He was upset. Maybe by the realization that Idalia's sudden affection for him had all the sincerity of the AOL voice that says, "Welcome." Maybe by the injustice of living beings in the likeness of humans who had no real purpose, no hope of a purpose. Knowing Jalil, probably that last thing.

"Watch this: Idalia? What is two plus two?"

Idalia blinked.

"I have two trees. I add two more trees. Now how many trees do I have?"

"Where are these trees?"

"MTV veejay material there," Christopher said.

How long he'd been awake and listening, I

couldn't guess. Not long or he'd never have been able to restrain some smart remark or other. "That's the career for her. Looks sexy but in a definitely weird way, and can't add two plus two. She's perfect."

He stood up. I noticed April stirring.

"Hey, there's a road down there."

"Yeah. It leads to Fairy Land," I said. "Has to be faster than traveling overland and we are in a hurry. I had to let you guys sleep, but we don't have any time to waste. Idalia says she can't go that way, though."

Those were the facts, more or less. I kind of felt it was up to Jalil to state the obvious conclusion.

He said, "Idalia, we have to travel fast. We only have six, well, five days now. So we have to take the road."

"But I cannot travel upon the road."

"Yeah, we know that," he said.

Idalia just smiled her green, empty-headed smile.

"What I'm saying is, we have to go, and you have to go back to the forest."

"But I love Jalil!"

Senna sighed, stood up, came over to us. "Go back to Iris. Her anger has cooled. Run to her, she's impatient."

There was a squeal and a green blur and Idalia was gone.

"You could have spent an hour trying to explain it to her," Senna said. "You don't have an hour to waste and anyway she'd never have gotten it."

"That was really awfully mean, Senna," April said.

"Sister, you were asleep so you missed the vital information: She's an automaton. She seduces mortal men, runs away from satyrs, that's it. The whole emotion is a programmed, automatic response from her."

"Why can't I meet a girl like that?" Christopher asked.

April said, "Love is programmed into her? You mean, as opposed to being a tool she uses to get her way? An illusion she creates with magic?"

"Senna's right," Jalil said, moving to cut off an April–Senna confrontation. "We never even really existed for her. What exists is right here." He tapped his chest. He didn't mean his heart. He meant the red stone.

We marched down to the road. I loosened my sword in its scabbard. No way to know what we were walking into. But time was short.

"Anyone asks, we're minstrels on our way to entertain the fairies," I said.

It was our basic cover story. We'd been a huge hit with the Vikings. Also in some nameless peasant hole in the deep forest. But Hel had not been amused. Maybe our luck would be better with the fairies.

We sauntered down looking as innocent as we could. At the same time we wanted to project a don't-mess-with-me look. It's a balancing act, Everworld is.

Part of me hoped for a fight. A fight I could win, anyway. Jalil had covered for me. Shown no expression when I lied to the others. But that left me feeling like a fake.

"Sheep coming up the road," Jalil said. "Let's hurry."

"Why hurry?" Christopher asked.

"You want to walk in front of the sheep or behind the sheep?"

"Ah."

We stepped up the pace and joined the road about fifty feet ahead of the first sheep. About the same distance behind a big oxcart loaded with what might be beets.

The road was hard-packed dirt and crushed shell. Like a country road down South. Grass faded at the edges. Intermittent knots of shade trees near the road offered temporary respite from the sun.

A stream, deep-cut and narrow, wound alongside the road. Reeds and cattails covered the banks.

For a while all we saw were the sheep behind us and the back of the oxcart ahead of us. And little enough of either of those. Jalil's hurry to avoid sheep crap had overlooked one vital fact: An awful lot of flocks had already moved along this road. We mostly kept our eyes down, looking to avoid the bigger piles. I was wearing the last pair of running shoes I'd ever find in Everworld. If they became unwearable it was lace-up boots if I was lucky.

Gradually we moved up on the wagonload of beets. But just as we were looking to pass, we ran into oncoming traffic. A file of dwarfs, an even dozen of them carrying huge sacks on their backs. The loads would have crushed a human. The dwarfs were sweating profusely and straining, but I heard no grumbling as they passed by.

It was my second view of dwarfs. The first time had been in Hel's harem city. They were taciturn creatures. A hair taller than Idalia definitely, but built as broad as they were tall. They might have been carved out of live oak. Despite the heat and their burden, each wore a chain mail shirt that went down to his knees and some sort of weapon: short sword, ax, nailed club.

The dwarfs seemed to have no interest in us. We decided to show none in them. I had the feeling that dwarfs liked to be left alone. I also had the feeling that if they weren't left alone the person who hassled them would be sorry.

We walked for another two hours, keeping as quick a pace as we could manage. The peaches had helped but not much. We'd had about a two-day food deficit. Water was plentiful but the food situation was becoming critical. I was thinking about dropping back to the beet wagon we'd passed and seeing if I could bargain for some. Had no idea what raw beets tasted like, or even if they could be eaten. But the hungrier I got the more open-minded I became.

The countryside was becoming prettier all the time. It had been nice to begin with: rolling hills, bands of trees broken up by flower-filled meadows. But now it was going beyond anything nature could manage unaided. We were walking through land that was more and more like a tended garden.

A low stone wall now lined the road on both sides. The shade trees lined up on both sides of the road, spaced far enough apart to allow for lush hydrangea hedges, orange daylilies, rosebushes bearing fat, full roses in white, pink, and red.

The grass was trimmed, edged, and as green and fresh as a golf course.

"Hey, I think my grandfather lives here," Christopher said. "This is exactly like his country club down in Florida. Less humid here. Not as many people driving with the turn signal on."

The only thing that marred the trimmed, artificial perfection was the sight of the satyr's legs bounding along.

"Man, what is going on with that?" Christopher wondered.

"It must feel some affinity for us. Maybe some inchoate attraction," Jalil suggested.

"It has no eyes," April pointed out. "How does it follow us? I mean, it has no head. No nothing."

"You know, I think on the scale of mysteries, how it follows us is maybe less mysterious than the mere fact that it can move at all," Jalil pointed out.

"Jalil, you talk so purty when you want to," Christopher said. "When you do that I feel an inchoate attraction for you."

The road turned around a willow so huge it seemed to be a small grove rather than a single tree. The road turned and we found ourselves looking at a gate.

It was very pretty. An arch formed out of rosebushes rose very high over the road. It would be just high enough for the beet wagon to squeeze under when it caught up to us. The arch was anchored on either side of the road by a stout stone wall. The wall extended maybe a hundred feet to the left and right and ended in a round stone tower two dozen feet tall, give or take. More roses adorned the top of the wall.

"That's pretty with all the roses," April said. "Kind of looks like what you'd expect the entrance to Fairy Land to be, huh?"

"It's not about the roses," I said. "It's about the

thorns. Try going over that wall — it'd be like barbed wire. And see on either side, out past the towers, more bushes of different types. I'm betting on more thorns. See the way the ground rises sharply? Someone wants to avoid this gate, they're going up a steep hill into dense thornbushes and with that tower looking down at them the whole time."

We approached the gate cautiously but without looking guilty or like we were worried. Senna's warning about little people who survived in a land of giants was fresh in my memory. And if I had forgotten it, this beautiful-yet-serious gate would have reminded me.

A small person lounged beside the gate, tipped back on a chair. He was smoking a long pipe. He wore a bright red cap, a bright green tunic, and soft shoes that ended in curled, pointed toes.

He was approximately the same size as a dwarf but built in more nearly human proportions. His legs were perhaps a bit short for his body, but other than that he could have been a seven-year-old with an old man's wrinkled, good-natured face.

As he spotted us he lifted his cap in greeting. Smiled around his pipe. Winked a blue eye.

"It's like right out of a fairy story," April marveled. "My great-grandmother, may she rest in peace, she was from Ireland, she'd tell stories about the leprechauns. They were just like that! Exactly. It's exactly the image I had in my mind from when I was little."

"Top o' the afternoon to ye, then, good folk," the leprechaun said. "And ladies, sure your loveliness pales the most beautiful rose on the bush. It does, it does, an' no mistake."

"Hello," I said. "We're looking for Fairy Land. I guess we're there, huh?" It was hard to feel very worried under the circumstances.

"You've found it, then, so ye have. Aye, you've found us out. How is it we can help you, good sir?"

"Well, we're traveling minstrels. We're looking to find a place to put on a show."

The leprechaun smiled. "Minstrels, are ye? Ah, then that's something, eh? Minstrels. Have you happened to notice as you walked along the road, I say have you happened to notice that from time to time you came upon, perhaps even stepped in, a steaming great pile of manure?"

I nodded, grinning, couldn't help myself. He was cute. And I don't use the word cute.

"Did you notice that, then?" The leprechaun grinned right back at me. Suddenly the smile evaporated. "Then you know what I think of your story of being minstrels. It's a steaming great pile of manure."

The little man rested in his chair and took a drag on his pipe.

"Did he just say bull product?" Christopher said.

"Bull if ye will. But horse, pig, sheep, ox, cow, and goat manure will do just as well. If you're minstrels, then I'm bleedin' Cuchulainn."

"Well, that's your opinion," I said. "Anyway, we'd like to get going."

"Would you? Would you, then? And how about the entrance tax?"

"The entrance tax?" I glanced back and saw that the beet wagon was slowly catching up to us. It was a stupid thing to be worrying about but I didn't want to hold up the line.

"Aye, the entrance tax. Who do you think pays for all the loveliness you see around you, eh? Who do you suppose pays me my salary to sit here all the long day playing the part? Me in my bright red cap and stockings and pointy shoes, do you suppose it's all free? Do you think I sit here choking on this damned pipe and dressed like some Old World pixie for my health? And what the bloody hell is that?"

He stood up and pointed to the half-a-satyr. Sandy's lower half had just plowed into the wall on our right.

"What is that mad thing?" he demanded. "It's following you, and it with no eyes, nor face to put eyes in, nor even a head, nor shoulders to put a head on."

My mouth was dry. This wasn't going as planned. He'd dismissed our cover story. And the happy fairy act had definitely been dropped.

April answered for us. "It's the bottom half of a satyr."

The leprechaun jerked visibly. He stared at April. Stared at me. "The bottom half of a satyr? What are you doing with the bottom half of a satyr?"

I started to answer but Christopher jumped in smoothly. "You like it? Maybe we could make a deal."

The leprechaun got a car-dealer look in his blue eyes. "I've seen better half-a-satyrs."

"No you haven't," Christopher said firmly. "This is top-of-the-line half-a-satyr."

The fairy bit his lower lip and muttered to himself. "I've no place to keep it. I could stick it in the shed for a while, maybe, but it'd be running into the walls keeping me awake all night. I'd have to trade it away soon as could be."

"We'll trade you the half-a-satyr for the entrance tax," Christopher said.

"Done," the leprechaun said. He still looked worried, like he was trying to figure out where to stick the running goat legs. "Still, it won't eat much, eh?"

"So we can go on in?" Jalil asked.

"Are you heading to the city or just as far as the market?"

"The city," I said for no special reason. "Can we go now?"

"That you may, though how you'll pay your way in the city without your half-a-satyr I'm sure I can't say." He reverted to his act. "Be off wi' ye, then, good lords and ladies, and the blessings o' the fairy folk upon your lovely heads."

Then, as we walked through the gate he yelled in a very different voice, "Sergeant! Send some of your boys out to grab my half-a-satyr. No more than two, I'm not paying extra!"

There was a guardhouse just past the gate. Two

fairies zipped past. They moved swiftly, though not quite at Idalia's breakneck pace.

They wore leather tunics and tight-fitting steel helmets. They carried bows and arrows and small swords.

They weren't large. Their weapons were child-sized. They looked almost comical. But I reminded myself not to underestimate these people.

It wasn't rosebush hedges that kept Nidhoggr at bay.

Inside the gate the grounds became even more carefully tended. Every bush perfectly shaped. Not a yellow blade of grass to be seen. Not a shaggy border, not a diseased tree.

The dirt and shell road was paved with yellowish bricks set in a herringbone pattern.

"Yellow bricks."

I said, "All right, Christopher, just get it over with."

"I have no idea what you're talking about."

"Uh-huh."

"You think I would stoop to some obvious *Wizard of Oz* joke at a time like this? That's kind of insulting, really. You think what? I'm going to say, 'Follow the yellow brick road' in a Munchkin voice?"

"It occurred to me."

"Yeah, well, give me some credit."

"Sorry."

"So. Senna. This must feel like home to you, huh? Where do you keep the flying monkeys?"

Christopher laughed, vastly amused by himself. To his amazement and mine, Senna actually answered.

"That was always my favorite movie when I was little."

"You were probably the only kid who ever thought the Wicked Witch of the West was the hero."

"It was the color shift. That's what I liked. The beginning of the movie is all in black and white. Gray, really. Then the tornado, and she wakes up in Oz. And suddenly it's all in color." Senna cast a cool, sidelong look at her half sister. "Some people see that and they're Toto, off and running, ready to go. Other people are Dorothy. They go to a fantastic new world and can't stop whining about Kansas."

April laughed. She'd been stung but not as badly as Senna had hoped. "I see, so we should be grateful to you for all this? I hadn't realized you were doing it all to be nice. I didn't realize you just wanted us to have a good time. See, I thought you were just dragging us into your little psychodrama so you could use us whenever it suited your purpose. Use us to distract and delay Loki.

Use us to fight dragons for you. Sell us out to your girlfriend Hel —"

"Shut up, you silly cow," Senna snapped in a voice like a knife.

We stopped walking. The blood drained out of April's face. Her lower lip was trembling but not in preparation for crying. Her teeth were bared, her eyes slits.

I'd never seen April mad. Not like this. I backed up a couple of steps without thinking.

Senna's face was all cold contempt. She was not afraid of April. She stepped right up to her sister, stepped up like some guy getting ready to throw down.

"You were there for hours. I was there for days," Senna said in a low, grating voice. "She hung me there, hung me there tied to a stake, facedown over that pit, sister, facedown looking at all those men down there in the shaft, hundreds, thousands of them, screaming night and day, crying, moaning, begging."

April said nothing, just stared, all the rage leaking away, replaced by amazement, incomprehension.

"I was there when they would drag the new ones down, that's when it's worst," Senna said. "The new ones, still fouling themselves from terror of Hel, and then her creatures drag them down to the pit, down along the serpent's coils and they see what awaits them. They see the corpses that are still moving. They see the living men little more than skeletons but dusty with cobwebs that took a hundred years to form. They see all that and they cry for their mothers, April. They scream, 'Mother, mother, mother, help me!' for hours and hours and scream and scream and —"

"Shut up!" Christopher yelled. "Just shut up. Shut up."

"It's so neat and easy for you, isn't it, April? It always has been. Good and evil. The good ascend to heaven, the evil burn in hell. Isn't that it, April? Isn't that the formula? And what am I, April? Evil? Surely you don't think I'm good. So as I hung there, I cried, yes, I cried. Yes, I screamed and begged. Yes, I wished I could die. And all the while I'm remembering my smug half sister and knowing that you thought I deserved it all."

Senna was panting, shaking. Sweat beaded on her forehead. I wanted to hold her, take her in my arms. But she was past that. Untouchable. Exalted.

Christopher was holding his head like he could squeeze out all the memories.

It was frightening how easily it could all be uncovered. When would those memories ever be watered down and lose their power? Never. No trick of mind would ever clean my memory.

I slowly unclenched my fist. Forced myself to take a breath. Of course Senna had been terrified. I should have seen that. She was human, after all, not some monster. She was like us, different, but still one of us.

"Nicely done, Senna," Jalil said.

I didn't believe my ears. I looked at him. Yes, he was unmoved. He was slowly shaking his head in, what, ironic admiration?

"Well done all the way, Senna," Jalil said. "Perfect timing, just when no one is expecting it. Perfect opening. You set us up with happy girlhood memories of going off to see the wizard, and then wham, down comes the hammer. Or should I say, in goes the wedge?"

Senna shook her head, too tired, too emotional to answer, to defend herself.

"Leave her alone, Jalil, you don't know what you're talking about," I said.

"You peeled off April as the poor old stick-in-the-mud who didn't understand how cool it was to be in this Technicolor world, then you bang the wedge in with some sob stories. You make April look like an insensitive, self-righteous jerk, and you? You're poor pitiful Senna with David as your protector."

"Damn it, Jalil, knock it off!" I yelled.

He smirked. "Perfect, isn't it? See, we were getting along too well. Now April's been demonized, David has stepped back into his role as Senna's boy, I look like a coldhearted creep, and Christopher's been punished for giving the witch grief. She's so good she should be teaching this stuff."

Was that a shadow of a smile on Senna's lips? No, surely not. No. There were real tears in her eyes. She was one of us, in the end.

And yet, a nagging voice reminded me as I unconsciously pressed my hand to my silent chest, there were four rubies. Not five.

Too pretty. That's what I kept thinking. Too neat, too orderly, too well kept. The yellow bricks had even been cleaned of manure. They sparkled, wet with a recent washing.

Fairy Land. It looked like Fairy Land. It looked like a gardener's heaven. There weren't five or six different types of flowers, there were hundreds. Tall, short, thin, plush, red, yellow, orange, green, white, pink, purple, even blue.

It reminded me of the Chicago Botanical Gardens where we'd gone in ninth grade on a field trip.

In fact the only dirty, shabby, disreputable-looking things were the travelers on the road, coming and going. And we looked as skanky as the rest. I became increasingly self-conscious about the fact that we were filthy and smelled as bad as any of the flocks of sheep. No part of me was clean. Hadn't been since long before our hike through Hel's world. I stank of stale fear-sweat.

No one was talking. Not since the blowup. And we were walking differently. April and Jalil close. Christopher out in front, like he was trying to outrun the rest of us, trying not to notice us and be reminded. Me and Senna.

Me and Senna, walking in silence, not close enough to be close, not far enough apart for the others to avoid seeing that we were together.

I was a damned idiot. That's what was so sad: I knew it. The witch didn't even have a word of kindness for me. No thanks. No "David, thanks for standing up for me."

She could have smiled. Could have reached for me, touched my hand, could have . . . didn't. Didn't need to, the cynical part of me said. She owned me. She knew she owned me.

If I was a leader I was doing a piss-poor job. We were fragmented, disunited. And I was just one of the fragments. We seemed incapable of working together. Each of us was a unit, none of us part of a team.

"Yeah, well, it isn't a football game, is it?" I muttered under my breath.

We topped a gentle hill and saw that the road ahead forked. One road left, one right. The end of neither could be seen as the fork was at the bottom of a dell.

"A sign," Christopher said, pointing. "There's an actual sign. Screw it, man, I'm staying here in Fairy Land; these are the first people yet who have the sense to put up a sign."

"What's it say?" I asked.

"Says, I swear, 'Yon City,' and an arrow pointing left, and 'Ye Marketplace,' and an arrow pointing right." He stopped and grinned. "Yon City is three miles, dude. Ye Marketplace is half a mile. Mileage. They put up the mileage. I love these guys. They have signs, they keep stuff clean, they do deals. I am prepared to convert to fairy."

"The market's closer," Jalil pointed out. "A lot closer."

"See? I always said you were a genius, Jalil," Christopher said. "Three miles, half a mile. E equals MC squared."

"My point was that we need food. We could use some clothing. We could use a bath. If the market is one place and the city is another, maybe that means we can't get anything in the city. I'm just guessing. Besides, everyone is going to the market. Look."

He was right. The slow foot and wagon and sheep traffic was all turning off toward the market.

"I told the guy we were going to the city. It seemed to fit with the whole minstrel cover story."

April said, "He didn't believe that anyway. Jalil's right, maybe we need a trip to the mall."

"Should we take a vote or is David going to do his Moses thing?" Christopher asked. "Hey, Senna? What's David going to say?"

I bit back the first angry shot that came to my mind. As calmly as I could I said, "I agree with Jalil and April." Senna, thankfully, said nothing.

We turned right at the fork. Long before we reached it we saw the marketplace. It was, to put it mildly, different from the fastidiously neat, well-ordered Fairy Land we'd gotten used to.

"That is the biggest damn garage sale I've ever seen," Christopher said.

It covered acres. Maybe a square mile but forming a rough, unkempt circle. At the center was an open space, a traffic circle with avenues radiating out in every direction. Connecting the paved avenues was an irregular network of unpaved streets. And within each pie wedge and trapezoid thus formed were buildings ranging from lean-to stalls covered with red-, green-, or yellow-striped canvas, up through one-story shops, and here and there a few genuinely large buildings, two, three stories tall, ornately faced with rococo moldings and roofed in a sort of pale blue tile. Not always but generally the more low-rent places were farther out toward the boundaries of the market. The bigger places predominated at the center, giving the impression of a scale-model cityscape, with "skyscrapers" defining the "downtown."

If there was any other organization to the place it seemed to involve keeping most of the beasts, the sheep, cows, pigs, and horses, in what could be considered the northeast quadrant.

The road we were on led to the market. Another road led out, presumably heading off to the unseen city.

Within the market the avenues and streets were choked with people. From this distance it was hard to be sure what type of people, but even at a distance I could see that they ranged widely in size, shape, and color.

The beet wagon was gaining on us again. We started moving. I was feeling better. We all were. Hard to imagine anything very terrible happening at the mall.

To our relief there was no gatekeeper charging an entrance tax for the market. We pushed through a knot of dwarfs bargaining with a pair of Coo-Hatch and headed down the avenue.

The late-afternoon sun was hot without being

brutal. Shadows were long and cool. We were walking by a long row of prepared food and drink. It made sense, of course; people just getting in from the road would want to eat and drink. We did.

"Little problem, General," Christopher said to me. "We have no money."

"Actually, we do," Jalil said. "I don't know about you guys but I still have the pocket change I had when we first got here." He dug the money out of his pockets, along with sand and a dead beetle.

"What's that, a snack?"

"Eleven bucks in paper, a quarter, a dime, and five pennies," Jalil reported. "But I doubt U.S. currency is going to be worth much here."

"Should have picked up a few things while we were standing around on Nidhoggr's treasure."

"Yeah, that would have been a good idea," April said with unusual sarcasm. "It's not like he notices anyone stealing from him. Why are we on this stupid trip? Because he wants some bowl he lost."

"I have a suggestion," Senna said quietly. "How about watching what you say? We're in a public place."

I looked around, suddenly aware that she was right. No one seemed to be within earshot, or to have overheard, but who could tell for sure? Nidhoggr was not a name a person was likely to confuse with something else.

We were on a mission, a possibly dangerous mission, and I'd already made a mistake. It made me mad. At Christopher and April.

"Both of you keep quiet," I said with more heat than I'd intended. "Jalil, let's try and buy some food."

Jalil nodded. He looked around and chose a stall selling what were hopefully sausages wrapped in pastry. The vendor was a human. That seemed like a good start.

"Be sure and get mustard," Christopher called after us.

"What'll you have?" the vendor asked, sounding like any counterman at any Gold Coast Dogs back home.

"Well, we'd like five of . . . those." He pointed.

"What'll you give?"

"Eleven dollars and forty cents."

The vendor was a big man, with huge hairy Popeye forearms, slicked-back hair, and an arrangement of teeth that seemed haphazard.

He picked up the single dollar bill and the two fives, plucking them daintily from Jalil's palm. He examined them closely, turned each over to look at the back.

"Who is this fellow?"

"That's George Washington. The other one is Abraham Lincoln."

The vendor pushed them back. "You may trade those to the scribes up on Poseidon Street. No good here."

"How about the coins?"

The man sucked his several teeth. "Any fool can see that's not solid silver. And those are coppers. One meat pie for the lot."

I called Christopher over and he and I dug for our own change. We produced five more quarters, a nickel, and four pennies.

A few seconds later we were focused on the question of how to divide three meat pies among five people.

"Some mustard, some relish, a big old dill pickle, some onions, hot peppers maybe, you'd have something," Christopher said as he finished his half plus a sliver of meat. "Fries and a Coke, too."

April said, "Yeah, and then throw on a salad, and a lemon seitan from Blind Faith Cafe and you'd really have something."

"You're going to tell me you actually fantasize about vegetarian stuff?" I said, trying to joke and make up for having dumped on April earlier.

"Yeah, whenever I'm not fantasizing about not seeing you for a good, long week or so."

"I'm still hungry," Christopher said. "We still have the junk in April's backpack. Poetry book, notebook, pen and pencils. The Discman. Her lame CDs. Got a bunch of keys and a couple of credit cards."

"Advil," April said.

"You have Advil?" Senna demanded eagerly.

"Cramps?"

"In a couple days," Senna admitted.

April smirked. "What do you know? I finally have something you want."

"We need a place to stay, more food, some clothing," Jalil summarized. "And we are in the middle of unrestrained capitalism here. We may be able to trade some of our stuff, but maybe we should be thinking more long-term."

"We have five days," I reminded him. "Three and a half if you give us time to get back to . . . to Large and Crusty. We're not moving in here."

But Christopher was intrigued. "What are you thinking, man? We go into business here?"

Jalil gave his patented sidelong look and smiled his little smirk. "So much we know they don't know. These people are sitting around stuck in the first millennium A.D.; we're on the verge of the third."

"Let's keep moving," I said, for lack of anything better to say. I was clueless, something I'd admit to myself but didn't want to admit to everyone. A stone, a sword, a spear, and a cauldron. That's what we were after. And they were somewhere in Fairy Land. But Fairy Land wasn't some Sleeping Beauty castle from Disney World, it covered a lot of ground, and finding four particular objects even in just this vast, endless, open-air market seemed impossible. It would take years of searching. And that's if whoever had them wasn't hiding them very well.

Wait. No. Of course. The fairies weren't hiding them. Jalil was right: These were capitalists.

"Let's move," I said with more certainty.

"Where the hell are we going?"

"The center of this market. Before the sun goes down."

# Chapter XIV

We passed blacksmiths. We passed butchers. We passed potters. We passed jewelers. Rope makers. Goldsmiths. Weavers. Cobblers. Armorers. Glassblowers. Coopers, carpenters, upholsterers, locksmiths, tanners, herbalists, fortune tellers, bakers, brewers, and some vendors, quite a few really, who defied any sort of sensible label.

If we'd had enough money we could have bought unicorn colts, rocs' eggs, love potions, flying snakes, eight-legged horses all supposedly descended from the true Sleipnir, whatever that was. I spotted at least three allegedly genuine hammers of Thor. We could, had we wanted, have paid for prostitutes or bought slaves.

We saw jugglers, mimes, tightrope walkers, sword swallowers, fire-eaters, bear wrestlers, python wrestlers, and troll wrestlers.

We could have dined on everything from corn on the cob to cheese to chickens.

If it existed in Everworld, I suspected it was here.

And if it lived in Everworld it was here, too. Dwarfs, men, elves, trolls, minor gods, a dozen different types of little people, talking animals, giants, Coo-Hatch, and at least three other species of aliens.

And all of them buying, selling, bargaining, threatening, cajoling, dealing, laughing, shaking hands, kissing cheeks, grasping arms, and spitting in palms.

Everywhere, everywhere, fairies in neat, dark blue tunics moved among stalls armed only with leather-bound notebooks on which they took careful notes.

"It's the fairy IRS, man," Jalil said. "They're getting a piece of everything."

Other fairies, fewer in number and wearing black, sauntered along alone or in pairs. It didn't matter that they were four feet tall, or that their skinny legs were enclosed in yellow tights, or that their weapons were half-sized swords and short horn-and-hide bows: They were cops.

We at last reached the center of the maze, beneath the welcome shade of tall buildings that reminded me vaguely of Mardi Gras in downtown

New Orleans. Not that I'd been there, I'd just seen pictures. There were balconies running the length of each building, and the trading went on, fairies mostly now, yelling down to elves or men or dwarfs or aliens in the streets below.

This was the nerve center. Here the trades were less tangible. Here they traded large quantities, thousands of bushels of wheat or hundreds of head of cattle. They were trading options and futures, betting on prices themselves.

"This is the first place in Everworld I've ever thought I could be happy," Christopher said. "See, this is real. This is money. This is business. Damn it, this is America."

"Don't get too comfortable," I said. I spotted a parked, empty wagon. I leaped up onto the back, formed my hands into a trumpet, and yelled, "We're here for the stone, the sword, the spear, and the cauldron of the Daghdha. We'll pay any fair price, and we —"

The black-tunicked fairies appeared from nowhere, moving at a speed that defied belief. They weren't big. But when something not big hits you fast enough, it's big enough.

I was off the wagon, on the ground, head ringing from the impact, sucking wind before I knew what had happened.

Three slender arrows held quivering against

three tight-drawn bows were within one foot of my heart.

I thought the joke would be on them: I had no heart. But six other arrowheads were milliseconds from piercing my eyes, stomach, and elsewhere.

Cautiously, carefully, slowly, I turned my head. The others were still standing. But they, like me, were a harsh word away from being pincushions.

A fairy wearing buff-colored clothes and a green hat stood over me, looking calmly down at me, smoking a pipe. He carried a tall walking stick with a massive gold knob on the top.

"I was just trying to do some business," I said respectfully.

"No better place in all of Everworld. This is the place for business," he said, nodding. "But a very poor place to go saying things best left unsaid."

"I . . . Sorry, but I . . . I can't say what I —"

"No," he said. "You cannot."

He swung the gold knob. I barely registered the blur of motion, then I was out.

# Chapter XV

I spent an anxious hour in English comp, then suddenly I was back.

Back in a mess.

I was seated in a chair that would have been appropriate for a day-care class. I was slumped forward, head down between my knees.

I jerked upward, felt a wave of dizziness and nausea sweep over me. The room swirled into view. I saw a throne on a dais. That had never been good news: Loki and Hel both had thrones. Huitzilopoctli had something close. Thrones were trouble; no one in this lunatic asylum was Prince Charles.

Glanced left and right. The others were all seated on chairs similar to mine. All conscious. All looking grim.

My sword was gone.

A dozen or more black-clad fairies stood at attention. They had a tough, capable look. Anyway, as tough as they could look and be four feet tall.

On the throne sat an old fairy, a leprechaun, I guess, since he looked like the guy at the gate. He wore a tall gold crown encrusted with jewels. In his hand he held a gold scepter, likewise covered in diamonds, rubies, and emeralds.

I didn't need a program to figure out that he was the king. A rich king. The walls, the ceiling, the floor, the furniture all looked like Nidhoggr's treasure had exploded and blown gold, silver, diamond, and emerald shrapnel everywhere.

Beside the fairy king, on a slightly smaller throne, sat the queen. She was a nice-looking older woman. No nymph or elf maiden. Just a size-extra-small, middle-aged woman with sharp eyes and a downturned, frowning mouth.

All of that was bad enough. But standing off in one corner was a creature unlike anything that had ever played a role in the collective unconscious of Homo sapiens.

He was taller than the fairies but just as slightly built. His eyes were those of an exceedingly large fly. He had wings folded against his back. His mouth was ringed by three small, jointed arms that seemed never to stop reaching for and grasping invisible food from the air.

"Hetwan," I gasped.

We'd seen this Hetwan, or another just like it, in the court of Loki. The Hetwan were the adherents of Ka Anor. And Ka Anor was not good news for anyone.

The truth jumped out at me in a flash. "It's all a damned setup."

"Very good, David," Jalil said with a mixture of actual approval and savage, angry sarcasm.

The fairy king spoke. "This is your leader?"

Idiotic as it was, I was gratified. The others must have identified me as their leader. Pathetic. More pathetic still once I realized the fairy had just reached that conclusion based on the fact that only I had been carrying a sword.

I spotted the sword leaning against a side door. I thought I also spotted a fairy guard nursing a burned hand. Galahad's sword burned any who took it without its owner's permission.

Nice to know it was still within reach. But I'm a realist. I might beat a troll in a quick draw, but when it came to the fairies I was a snail. I'd have every arrow in every quiver in the room sticking out of me, and the fairies would be off having a smoke before I made it halfway to the sword.

The fairy captain, the guy who'd nailed me with the gold-headed cane, must have seen me thinking it over. He raised one finger, shook it back and forth, and mouthed the word, "No."

"I'm the leader," I said to the king. "My name is David Levin."

"You are a spy."

"No, your honor. I mean, Your Highness."

There was the sound of blade hitting wood.

I hadn't seen the archer move. I didn't see anything except the arrow that pierced the inseam of my pants and stuck into the wooden chair leg.

I stopped breathing.

"You are a spy," the king repeated. "Nidhoggr's spy."

"I'm not Nidhoggr's spy, I —"

An arrow appeared a quarter inch to the left of the first arrow. It took a few seconds for the pain to reach my head. Just a flesh wound, a superficial cut. But the message was crystal clear: These fairies could skin me alive if they wanted. They were that fast, that good. And I was that big, dumb, and slow.

I was sweating. It was starting to roll down into my eyes.

The king said, "You are —"

I should have kept my mouth shut, or better yet agreed. "Dammit, you can shoot arrows into me all day, we were sent by Nidhoggr, yes, yes, but we aren't spies."

"What he means is that while we are not spies," Jalil said smoothly, "we are thieves."

The king looked ready to order a matched set of arrows for my eyes. But the queen put her hand on his leg.

"Truth," she said.

The king looked surprised but not skeptical.

The queen leaned toward us and said, "The dragon sent you to steal the treasures of the Daghdha? Not to merely learn their location?"

"He didn't say we should report back. He said we should get the stuff. Four things. Then we were supposed to bring them back to him."

The Hetwan stared, unblinking, emotionless as far as I could tell. If it recognized us it didn't let on. Maybe all humans looked the same. Most likely this was a different Hetwan.

The question was not whether he recognized us, but whether he knew who and what Senna was. Hetwan power had helped Loki bring Senna across the barrier between universes. The gateway was supposed to be Hetwan property. Loki had intended to doublecross them and use Senna himself.

Give up Senna to the Hetwan and we could probably walk away free. I knew it. Jalil almost certainly knew it. April? Maybe. Would she sell out her half sister? No, April wouldn't open the gateway between worlds and let the horrors of Everworld spill into her precious real world.

But Christopher would. And I couldn't let him.

"It was a trap, wasn't it?" I asked. "You sent in a team to steal from Nidhoggr. You wanted him to come after it."

"They wanted Nidhoggr to come after it?" Christopher shrilled. "No one wants Nidhoggr coming after anything! Have you people ever seen him?"

The queen almost laughed. Her husband looked shamefaced. Obviously this had been his idea. A fact that could be useful to me. If I lived long enough to use it.

"What did Nidhoggr agree to pay you for stealing from us?" the king asked.

I decided to try the truth. "He took our hearts. He replaced them with . . . with rubies. In a few days the rubies will catch fire and kill us. Unless we bring him the stone, the sword, the spear, and the cauldron of the Daghdha."

The queen did laugh this time. "He can have the cauldron, for all I care. The magic cauldron that never fails to provide food? No one goes to the cauldron and comes away hungry, no matter how many times, how many men. It is always full." She lowered her voice to a conspiratorial whisper. "What they don't tell you is that the food it supplies in such abundance is garbage."

"It needed salt," her husband grumbled.

"Needed salt? It wasn't fit to feed a human, much less any self-respecting fairy. Boiled cabbage and half-rotted beef. They're using it for the pigs, and the better class of pig refuses it!"

"Corned beef and cabbage?" April whispered.

"Irish food," Christopher muttered.

"So," the queen summarized, "Nidhoggr is not so great a fool that he fails to smell the trap you have laid. He does not come rushing in pursuit only to be skewered like a piece of mutton. Hah!"

The king turned, reluctantly I thought, to the Hetwan. "It would seem we have failed."

"Yes," the Hetwan agreed. "Ka Anor will not be pleased."

"We're all sensible folk here," the king said, spreading his hands wide in supplication. "We've done our best. We all lose by this, all lose equally."

"Ka Anor is not tolerant of loss," the Hetwan said.

"It's the fault of these human fools," the king said. "I'll have them killed immediately."

It all happened too fast for me to intervene, to say a word, to stop anything.

The king raised his hand.

The captain signaled his men.

In seconds we —

"No! We have the witch. We have the gateway to the Old World. They won't tell you, they'd rather die, but she is the witch Ka Anor seeks, the gateway."

The words were out before I could even think of shouting stop. And in any event I'd have been too stunned to react quickly.

It wasn't Christopher.

It was Senna.

She was on her feet, hand outstretched, finger pointing. Pointing at April. "There! There is the witch Loki brought from the Old World."

# Chapter XVI

There was a shocked, disbelieving silence.

"What would Ka Anor pay for this witch?" Senna asked the queen pointedly.

Too fast. She'd been perfect. Perfect. She'd chosen her moment, said the right words in the right way. We could deny April was the witch all day and night. Senna had already marked us as her protectors. We were suspect. Senna, as the informer, was not.

And what was worse was the realization that we could not give Senna up. Could not turn the accusation against her. We couldn't give Ka Anor the true gateway.

"The girl asks an interesting question," the queen drawled to the Hetwan. "What would Ka Anor pay?"

"The witch is Ka Anor's by right," the Hetwan began.

The queen cut him off with a rude noise. "This is the Fairy Kingdom, Hetwan. We do not cringe in terror every time your master's name is mentioned. Ka Anor eats gods, not mortals. And mortal we are, for better or worse. Which leaves us to contend only with Ka Anor's slaves. And how will Ka Anor feed all you Hetwan without our market?"

The Hetwan showed no reaction. He didn't argue the point.

"The witch is for sale," the queen said with a delighted laugh. "I doubt Ka Anor can pay as much as Nidhoggr's treasure, but I think he will pay well. Very, very well."

"It will take me some days to go to Ka Anor and hear his answer," the Hetwan said.

The queen waved her hand airily. "Take all the time you need. We will keep the witch safe and sound for you."

"David," April pleaded with me.

"Don't worry, we'll get you out," I whispered. "We can't give them what they want."

Her eyes flashed hatred. At me? At Senna? Maybe she didn't see any difference between us. She knew she was trapped. She knew I was right.

I hoped she knew I was telling the truth, that we would get her out.

"Take the witch to the dungeon, place her under triple guard, night and day," the king said, reasserting himself. "As for the others . . ." He glanced at his wife.

"The girl has bought their freedom. For now. But you Old Worlders should know that you may not leave our domain. If you try we will order you killed." To the fairy captain she said, "Give them their belongings and remove them. They smell."

April was dragged off. At least the guards were gentle. Maybe fearing her alleged powers. Maybe not wanting to damage their queen's property.

Fairy guards carried us from the room, literally carried us, probably impatient with our slowness. They pushed us out, threw April's backpack and my sword out after us, and slammed the palace door shut. Suddenly we were alone, just the four of us. April's absence was a larger fact than the presence of any of us.

We were standing outside the somehow smaller-than-expected door of an impressive and unusual castle built not of massive limestone blocks but of serpentine-patterned bricks overlaid with gold. Or maybe they were solid gold. The fairies didn't have Nidhoggr's astounding wealth, but they weren't on food stamps, either.

We were no longer in the marketplace. This had to be the city. Narrow streets, high walls, all perfectly clean, sterile even. We were the only humans on a street populated by swift, bustling fairies.

I was on guard, half expecting Jalil or Christopher to assault Senna. But it was me that Jalil turned on.

"Was that evidence enough for you, David? You think now maybe you can figure out what Senna's about?"

"You were seconds from being dead," Senna said calmly. "Now you're alive. Free. Thanks to me."

Jalil refused to look at her. He kept his angry face turned toward me. "She's right, you know. She's absolutely right. But that's not the point, is it, David? Do you see the truth about her? When it suited her she sold us out to Hel. When it suited her she sold April out."

True. Of course. But necessary. Much as I hated it, Senna had saved us while I was still fantasizing about grabbing my sword.

And yet, the ease with which Senna had made the choice to give April up. Couldn't ignore that. Couldn't pretend it hadn't made my insides squirm. If only I could talk to Senna.

Later. Now I had problems.

"What do you want from me, Jalil?" I demanded. "You want me to kill her? Is that it?"

Christopher said, "It sure would solve a lot of problems, wouldn't it?"

I yanked my sword from its scabbard. I held it out for Christopher. "Here. Do it."

"Screw you, David, she's your —"

"How about you, Jalil? Here. Here's the sword. Kill her."

For a long, horrible moment I thought Jalil might do it. But then his eyes wavered, looked away.

"I've had it with this crap," I ranted. "Whenever it's convenient you push me out front and say, 'Go, David, take over.'"

"Like I said, David, we aren't into going down with the *Titanic* just because you can't see the iceberg."

"You know what, Jalil? Then you carry the sword and do what needs doing. You want me to lead, then when it hits the fan you bail out on me. This goes both ways, man, both ways. You want a leader, then you have to follow. A little, at least. I never pretended to be perfect. I haven't lied to you and said, 'Follow me, I know what the hell I'm doing.' I don't know what the hell I'm doing. I'm in the middle of a tornado here and you're sitting there all smug saying, 'Hey, man, don't mess up.'"

"Okay, chill, dude, take it down a little," Christopher said. "People are looking at us."

The street was mostly empty. But some nearby black-suits were taking an interest in our argument. Night was falling fast and Fairy Land wasn't the kind of place where they put up with people shouting in the streets.

I lowered my voice. It wasn't easy. I was pissed. All the more because I was aware, aware in every brain cell, of my own failure. April taken prisoner. About to be sold off to Ka Anor. Guarded by little people I couldn't even think about challenging.

We had no weapons that could impress the fairies. Nothing. We were powerless. It's why the queen had cut us loose. The fairies thought they could handle Nidhoggr if he flew in, and maybe they could, they weren't fools. If they could handle Nidhoggr, if even the old dragon had realized that himself, what chance did we have?

In my chest was a stone that would burst into flame and kill me. Unless I stole from the fairies and somehow escaped. Only now, on top of that, I had to rescue April in the process.

"What the hell do we do?" I asked no one in particular. "What do we do?"

"These little turds were gonna nail Large and Crusty, man," Christopher said, echoing my own thoughts. "They were actually trying to draw him here."

Jalil sighed, letting go of his own anger. For now at least. "My guess is that it was a two-sided deal: The fairies set up Nidhoggr, get him out in the open. Then the Hetwan kill him. They must have some weapon. The fairies get his treasure, it's all they care about, and Ka Anor gets a clear path for his invasion of the Underworld."

"Businessmen, man," Christopher snorted appreciatively. "You have to give it up for these fairies. They will take risks for a dollar."

"They control and tax what is probably Everworld's premiere market. Sort of the New York Stock Exchange meets the Mega Mall," Jalil said. "I wonder if that's a weakness?"

"What?"

"Money. They are some greedy little creeps. If we could . . . I mean, is there anything they wouldn't do for money?"

"What are you going to do?" I scoffed. "Bribe the people who live in a gold castle? Get real. Buy Nidhoggr's stuff back?"

"Yeah, maybe," Jalil said. "Maybe that's exactly right. I mean, that's the thing about greed.

Enough is never enough. Even too much isn't enough."

"And what do we have to trade?"

Jalil shrugged.

"Out with it," Christopher prodded. "I've been watching you, Jalil. You got some idea back in the market. I heard gears turning in your head."

Jalil shrugged. "Back in the market I saw copper. Sheets and ingots. Copper wire, too. Not a lot, but it wouldn't take much."

"For what?" I asked.

Jalil slid me one of his sidelong looks. "To wire up the fairies."

I hesitated. It wasn't my plan. I didn't have a plan. It was Jalil's plan. But that wasn't the point, not really. The point was to climb up out of the hole we'd dug for ourselves. Whoever got the credit.

I looked at Senna. "Can you help us?"

"How? Use my magic to make the queen release us?" She shook her head. "Doubtful. One on one, maybe. But she's watched too closely. And anyway, women . . ." She shrugged. "Her husband, the king, yes, I could handle him if I could get close. But the queen is the real power."

I thought that over. "We need an investor. A venture capitalist. And we need protection. What do we have to sell? Telephones? What exactly are you thinking, Jalil?"

"Telegraph. That would be easiest. All you have to do is set up a key to interrupt the power. Couple of magnets. Some wire. A power source." He shook his head. "What am I even talking about, man? They don't have electricity."

"We can make electricity," I said. "I mean, we can, right?"

"Sure. A river or stream or whatever, a waterwheel. I'd need wire, I'd need trained carpenters, trained blacksmiths, or whatever."

"What do the fairies need with a telegraph?" Christopher asked. "Fast as they are?"

"They aren't faster than electricity."

"The market." I laughed. Maybe this was my idea after all, in part at least. "The money guys buying and selling near the center of the market? What are they buying and selling? Econ class: They're buying and selling commodities. Come on. To the market."

"Hey, I don't know about you, Bruce Wayne, but I'm beat," Christopher complained.

But Jalil's eyes were shining. All the anger between us was forgotten. There was the sound of awe in his voice. "Oh my god," he whispered. "Mr. Jones? My name is Mr. Dow. Pleased to meet you."

"What are you two even talking about?" Christopher demanded.

But he was talking to our backs. Jalil and I were on our way. If he followed, fine. If Senna followed, fine there, too.

But for the first time since before we'd reached Hel's city I felt like I had a clue.

It was a good long walk to the market and my optimism had faded long before we got there. Night will do that to you. Darkness eats optimism.

Halfway there we rested on a rise more or less equidistant between market and city. It was set up as a resting place. They had a neat, clean little outhouse, a couple of benches, and strategically placed shade trees that were obviously irrelevant to us.

Strangely, though, they had planted a tall hedge that blocked the view of the castle and the city. We could see the market, lights winking out one by one. But the city view was blocked.

I don't know why but this fact pissed me off. There was something a bit too Disney about Fairy Land. Too controlled.

I pulled out my sword and made a slash in the hedge. Vandalism, that's all it was. Anger turned into stupid action.

"That's right, get us busted for cutting up the plants," Christopher said as he exited the outhouse.

I ignored him. Pushed my head into the hedge, into the slash I'd made. They didn't want me to see the city, too bad, that was all the more reason for me.

It turned out to be a stunning view. The gold towers of the city glittered dimly in moonlight. There were lights on in the castle's keep. No doubt the fairy queen giving the king hell over his wasted plan to nail Nidhoggr.

"Shouldn't we get going?" Jalil said behind me.

"Yeah. We should." I pulled back, tried to fluff the stiff branches back in place to cover the damage I'd done. I felt disappointed. Weird, but I'd had the feeling there was something important to see. An instinct, maybe. Something. And now I had the feeling I'd missed something.

I looked again. The city. Towers, all round. Bigger ones gilded with crenellated roofs. Smaller ones clustered at the edge of the city, all topped with pointed roofs. I shook my head in wonder and puritanical disapproval: I'd swear the pointed roofs were tiled with diamonds.

We made it back to the market. It was late and shutting down. We traded our assorted house and car keys for a late dinner of mutton stew. The proprietor was about to throw the food out. I guess strange bits of brass were better than nothing.

Then we found a bare bit of ground under the awning of an apparently abandoned stall and slept.

I took first watch. I stayed awake this time. Jalil fell asleep as soon as he could, excited alternately by the prospect of becoming a wealthy mogul and of crossing over to do some research in the real world. Christopher was already asleep.

"I could take a watch," Senna said.

She was leaning back against one of the poles that held the tattered awning up.

"No," I said curtly.

Silence. Then, "She's fine. They'll take good care of her until the Hetwan returns. There'll be a bargaining process, probably over the course of days. They'll feed her, shelter her. She'll have a bed to sleep on."

I didn't have anything to say. I adjusted my clothes to be as comfortable as possible. It was cooling off fast now that the sun was down.

"Which is better, David, to do a harmful thing with the best of intentions? Or to do the useful thing, whatever your motivations?"

"I remember kissing you," I said. "I remember how it made me feel. Even with all that's happened, all the terrible things that are in my brain now, I remember every detail of kissing you."

"I remember it," she said.

"A million years ago. A million miles away."

We were sitting, facing each other, her knees drawn up, my legs crossed. A chill breeze ruffled her hair, blew golden strands forward across her gray eyes.

I shivered. From cold. From exhaustion. From memory.

"Sit here," she said. "Sit by me, David."

I felt the need for her. For warmth. For softness. For her lips on mine, for the magic that would soothe all my doubts away. I was cold inside and out. Sad and alone. The rush of the big plans had gone away when Jalil fell asleep. All I had now was the knowledge that I had lost one of us, lost April. That I was not trusted. That I had not found the way to save us.

I started to move toward Senna. Leaned forward and on hands and knees crawled to her. Not magic, not this time. Or at least a simpler magic. I wanted her. I wanted her to be real to me. I wanted that moment back when we had been side by side in the front seat of my car and every cell of me had wanted her. It had been uncomplicated then. Lust that was simply lust, and need that was only need. And love, maybe, yes, maybe love.

I would have crawled to her then, too, crawled and pressed my body against hers and my lips against hers and held and touched and demanded.

Now I crawled knowing there was no truth in it, knowing there would never be love, but crawling just the same because I was weak and she was strong and I wanted it to be that way. I had to go to her because I had to, that was all. Because she was where I had to be, because there was no going back.

She welcomed me, let me settle beside her, let me lean back against her shoulder, let my cheek rest against her, let me breathe her, let me glow with the power that came from her, let me close my eyes and imagine her in a different world.

She leaned down, raised my head just a little, and kissed me, and I thought, *Ah, then she is scared, she is worried, she does need me still, maybe just for a while.*

Her lips withered my strength. Her touch tightened the handcuffs. She had put the collar around my neck and held the leash in her hand.

I knew what she was doing. I knew she was binding me closer to her. I felt the ruthlessness of her will, never doubted it, never was fooled, never believed there was a moment of real feeling for me, and yet, and yet . . .

I knew that I had to choose. I could be my own man. Or hers.

She pushed me away. She wanted to sleep. I didn't resist. It was all part of the program. She wanted me to feel the sudden cold, the absence, the emptiness. She wanted me to feel how alone I was without her.

I felt it.

I felt.

But in my mind I saw towers.

From first light of dawn we stalked our prey. It wasn't hard. The fairies had no problem with ostentatious displays of wealth. The poor ones were wearing other people's uniforms: blue for tax collectors, black for cops, red for traders who worked directly for the "royals."

The rich fairies liked to dress the part. Fantastic outfits of red and purple, green and orange, feathers everywhere, fur trim, heavy gold chains, massive diamond rings.

We wanted someone with money. Someone young enough to still be on the make.

We found him working the inner ring, using silent hand signals to control his own boys, three guys who shouted orders for sheep, lumber, and copper.

Once we saw the interest in copper we knew we had our guy.

I approached him. He ignored me. I stood in his line of sight, blocking his view of his boys.

"Kindly step aside."

"Five seconds of your time."

He arched a brow. "For what purpose?"

"For the purpose of making you richer than the king."

He started to laugh. Caught himself. Looked sharply at me. "Are you mad or a fool?"

"Five seconds of your time, and you can decide that."

"What do you want?"

"I want you to place this small tip in your ear." I held the small earpiece of a set of headphones.

"Do you propose to work some magic on me?" he demanded.

"No magic. Better than magic: technology."

He jerked his head and a guy I hadn't noticed before came rushing over. To me he said, "This member of my staff will place his sword blade against your throat. If this is some sort of trick he will remove your head from your neck."

"Fair enough," I said.

The sword appeared. The blade was a millimeter from my jugular.

"Just place this in your ear, like I'm doing. See?"

The fairy raised the earpiece. Settled it in his ear. And heard a sound that had never been heard in Fairy Land before: Johann Sebastian Bach.

He jerked in surprise, then realized what he'd done and grabbed his retainer's sword hilt a split second before my head was doomed to go rolling.

Holding his man's hand, he listened. I handed him the other earpiece and he listened in stereo. And his eyes went wide. And his mouth hung open. And his face shone as if a light had come down from heaven to be his personal spotlight.

At last he took the earpieces out of his ears and looked greedily at the CD player I held.

"What will you take for this?"

I shook my head. "It's not for sale. Look, it will work maybe four hours before it goes dead. That was just to get your attention. Just to convince you to listen to our proposal."

"I'm listening."

Jalil stepped forward, with Christopher and Senna not far behind.

"We have a piece of technology," Jalil said. "It can communicate faster than the fastest fairy can run. It can send information over hundreds of miles instantaneously."

The fairy looked blank.

Christopher stepped in. "Mr. Fairy, what we're saying is that, look, you buy or sell some sheep, right? You buy a flock of sheep for a dollar and sell them for a dollar ten. Because you figure more sheep are coming, right? Coming to the market and they'll sell for the same price, give or take. But. But, what if you knew that there weren't going to be any sheep for a week, or a month? If you knew that, then you could charge more for your sheep, right? Law of supply and demand. More sheep mean cheaper sheep. Fewer sheep, more expensive sheep."

The fairy considered this for a moment. "Yes, this is true."

"So if you knew, knew for a fact that you had the only flock of sheep within fifty miles, hell, you could charge a lot more for sheep. Am I right?"

"How would I know such a thing was to occur?"

"It's called a telegraph. And that's only the beginning, my brother, because, see, the same technology can warn you if bad weather is coming or tell you if there's an enemy army heading your way. It can be used to send messages to your people far away."

It took another half hour to lay the whole thing out. To convince the fairy, whose name was

Ambrigar, that the CD player was not the thing that made it all happen. Even then he didn't get the whole magnitude of the deal we had for him.

"Yes, this would confer a great advantage on me in my trading business. If I knew what others did not, I —"

Christopher interrupted. "Dude. Ambrigar. The others will know it, too. Everyone will know. I mean everyone would want to know what the corn crop over in Cowtown is like, or whether there's a drought in Mootown, or how many wagonloads of beets are coming up the road. And everyone is going to want to be able to communicate with their brother or cousin or employee out in Trollville, right? Everyone is going to want this same power you'll have."

"Yes, but . . . then how . . ."

"You charge them."

"I . . ."

"The king wants to send a note to some other king? You charge the king a dollar. Some bread baker wants to order some special flour from Clodkicker City, you charge him a dollar. Some chick wants to send a love note to her love muffin way out on the frontier, wherever, you charge her a dollar." Christopher smiled. "That's where the money is, man. You can be AT&T and Dow Jones and AOL, all rolled into one."

"Everyone who wishes to use my magic wire . . ."

"You charge them a magic dollar."

"By the gods," the fairy whispered.

"That's right, my friend, you'll be able to buy the gods."

Then, and only then, did we tell him our price.

He stomped off. For an hour or so we thought we'd lost.

Then Ambrigar stomped back. "Show me this magic wire. Make it work. Prove this magic to me."

Jalil nodded. "We need carpenters, we need lumber, we need a small amount of iron or steel, a blacksmith, a jeweler, and a lot of copper wire."

"Copper wire? What they use for ear adornments for ladies?"

"Capitalism," Christopher said with a happy laugh. "It's a beautiful thing."

We surveyed the route we'd take. From a point on a fairly swift stream that ran more or less parallel to the fairy road, roughly a quarter mile to the near side of the marketplace. Ambrigar owned a small smithy there. Ambrigar owned quite a bit, it turned out.

But like Jalil had said, even too much wasn't enough. Ambrigar had the vision thing now. Ambrigar was smelling the cash.

Blacksmiths? He had blacksmiths. Jewelers? No problem. Copper wire, steel ingots, lumber, no problem at all. He promised us anything we needed.

Jalil was running the show. Jalil had some vague idea what he was doing, which was more than I had. Jalil was high. Jalil was whipping out diagrams and doing calculations, scribbling with blunt pieces of chalk on wooden planks or scraps of parchment.

"Fairies!" Jalil snapped at one point. "All the workmen have to be fairies. They'll speed things up. Humans won't do. Get me fairies!"

Ambrigar protested. Fairies would charge more. But Christopher was handling Ambrigar, building him up, hurrying him along, playing the salesman. Ambrigar agreed to hire fairies.

I grabbed Jalil at one point, almost had to shake him to get him to look up from a diagram he was drawing.

"What?" he snapped.

"Can we do it? Ticktock. Can we do it in time?"

He had a wild look in his eyes. "Yeah. We can. Maybe. Maybe if everything goes just right and you don't waste my time."

"Can I help?"

"What? No. Yes. Go into the market, find something nonconducting we can use to hold the wire. Like, uh, I don't know, like made out of pottery or porcelain maybe. Glass. Have to be able to thread a wire through them and attach them to a wooden pole. We need . . ." He tore through a few pages of paper covered with figures. "We need fifteen, minimum. Better double that if you can. Go!"

He pushed me away. Not angry, just mainlining adrenaline.

We were in the third day of a six-day countdown. Jalil had to construct a waterwheel that would generate current. String a wire along a quarter mile of poles that had yet to be cut or trimmed. Invent a couple of telegraph keys out of available materials. Do it all and leave enough time for us to ransom April, buy the Daghdha's stuff, and get back to Nidhoggr before the rubies in our chests turned into little volcanoes.

Assuming the ransom was big enough. Assuming somehow that we could outbid Ka Anor using Ambrigar's resources.

Assuming.

The unspoken but definite probability was that we might not be able to outbid Ka Anor. That was the problem. Ransom Nidhoggr's crap, save our own lives? Yeah, that, maybe. But April?

In our minds we'd already come to that point. We already knew, see. Subtly our efforts had become about saving our own asses, not rescuing April. But that couldn't be the way it was.

I cruised the market looking for I didn't know what, with one of Ambrigar's retainers shadowing me, ready to lay down cash for whatever I needed.

So we'd get the Daghdha's toys back to Nidhoggr. Maybe. And he'd give us back our hearts. Maybe. And April would be hauled off to Ka Anor, who would demand she do what she could not possibly do.

And on the sixth day her unexchanged ruby would burst into flames.

I noticed what looked like the same beet wagon we'd shadowed earlier on the way into fairy land. It was loaded up with various goods. Mostly rolled carpets piled high. They looked in a hurry to leave.

Past them I spotted an armorer. There were several trays laid out on a table. "Arrowheads," I said.

"Yes, but those are not the finest, perhaps," the armorer replied. "These are merely cheap porcelain, useful for hunting large game that may run off carrying a more expensive bronze arrowhead. But note the cunning placement of this small hole that allows them to be attached firmly to the shaft with a tiny nail that I also happen to sell."

"Yeah. I'll take thirty."

"Thirty! Then perhaps the good gentleman would care to see my lines of bronze arrowheads?"

"No, just those thirty, please. This guy will — ah-ah-ah! Of course!" I actually slapped my hands together in excitement at the sudden realization. "That's why they put up the hedge. Towers, my ass."

"Sir?"

"Nothing. Wrap 'em up." Hopefully my outburst hadn't been noticed. Ambrigar's retainer didn't seem interested. No one else, either. The armorer just wanted to sell me some arrowheads.

I got back to Jalil as quickly as possible. Strangely, he was trying to fall asleep inside a tent that had been put up near the river construction site.

"I need to cross over, back to the real world, check out some designs on some of this stuff. Christopher will wake me up two hours after I fall asleep."

"You could cross over and be in class."

"I can handle that. I'm more worried about being asleep over there and not being able to wake up."

"Listen, I think we need a plan B."

"Thanks for that vote of confidence."

"Jalil, be honest: If I told you I had a serious plan B would you tell me there's no way we'll need it?"

He shook his head. "No. Too much could go wrong with plan A. Everything could go wrong. So what's plan B?"

"Bring Nidhoggr here," I said.

"Good plan. Let's hope to hell plan A works."

"Look, Nidhoggr was suspicious that the fairies were setting him up, right? He figured if he showed up here looking for his stuff the fairies had some way of taking him down so they could grab the rest of his fortune. Right?"

"So far. I'm still waiting for the part where you get Large and Crusty to fly over here."

"Nidhoggr was right," I said, lowering my voice to a whisper. "The fairies were waiting. I saw these narrow towers back in the city, back in the palace itself. You wouldn't see them from the city streets, the walls of the castle are too high given the angle. But from the road where we stopped to take a leak? You can see them from there, and the fairies planted that big hedge to keep people from doing that."

"I don't have a lot of time, man," Jalil said, tapping an invisible watch.

"The towers are arrows. Huge arrows. Big enough to nail Nidhoggr. I don't know what they're using to launch them but that's what they are. Several of them. Nidhoggr would have come scoping down on the palace, on the city. They launch the towers, kill Nidhoggr, and bam, his whole treasure is up for grabs and the Hetwan don't have to watch their backs if they invade the Underworld."

Jalil didn't tell me I was full of it. Which worried me. I guess I'd been hoping he'd poke holes in my theory. Plan B was not going to be a party.

Jalil just said, "Okay, so you do what?"

"I sneak out of here, get back to him, and say, 'Look, man, you want your stuff? I know how you can make it safely in and out of fairy air space. I know how you can scare the fairies into giving up your stuff. Just one thing: We have something we want to get back, too.'"

"April."

"No one gets left behind."

Jalil nodded. Yawned. "You taking Senna?"

"Yeah. She's my responsibility."

Jalil laughed. "That's your curse, David: Everything is your responsibility."

I went back to the abandoned stall we'd made our unofficial home. Ambrigar had sent over some rugs for the ground, some pillows, and necessities.

Senna was outside the stall talking to a man in a leather apron. She had her hand on his arm. He was smiling a goofy half smile and chattering away.

"Say good-bye," I snapped. Was I jealous? No. I knew Senna was just using her unique power on the man. Making the contact that allowed her to lower the man's defenses and inhibitions.

It was what she did to me. Not jealousy, that's not what I felt. Embarrassment. Seeing my own weakness on that stranger's face. Like seeing a videotape of yourself drunk.

Senna followed me inside meekly enough.

"We have to get out of Fairy Land," I said.

"Do we?"

"Yeah. You have to come with me."

She raised her gray eyes to me. "I like it here. Merlin can't touch me here. Loki can't touch me here. I've been learning about this world-within-a-world. This marketplace is vital, and because of that it's treated as neutral territory. The gods leave it alone. Known wizards — or witches — are followed from the time they arrive, and unlike me, Merlin is well-known. I can stay here and learn all I need to know to . . . to go on with my life. I can make alliances. I can raise forces. This is as close to civilization as Everworld gets. I can grow stronger here. Strong enough to leave. But not now."

"You can come back here when I'm done," I said.

She frowned just a little. Like she couldn't quite understand me. "I'm not leaving, David. Neither are you. I need you. I need all of you, I see that now. Here you and Jalil can amass a fortune. I'll need that wealth to —"

"What makes you think we'd help you? Maybe me, maybe you think you have me whipped. But Jalil isn't going to do what you say."

"I think he will."

"And you know I will, huh? You know I'll do whatever you tell me."

"You love me," she said simply.

"I'm getting April out."

"Forget April. She's gone."

"Maybe you're right," I said.

I hooked my right arm upward from my waist, fist clenched. I caught Senna under the point of her chin. Her head snapped back. For a moment she wavered, eyes crazy, rolling, then her knees gave way.

I caught her as she fell.

"I love you," I whispered. "And maybe you do own me. But I'm getting everyone out of this alive. Even you."

I straightened her out, tied her hands behind her back, tied her ankles. Stuffed a wad of cotton cloth into her mouth and used more of the cloth to wrap around her head and hold the gag in place.

I dragged her into place and wrapped her up slowly, carefully, in the rug. I tied the rug. Checked to make sure she was getting air.

Then I hefted her onto one shoulder and set off in search of the former beet wagon I'd spotted earlier. Senna wasn't heavy. Neither was the rug. Together they weighed a ton. I was sweating by the time I got back to the wagon. It was already in motion.

I ran, huffing and wheezing and panting. I caught the tailgate and flung Senna aboard. Not gently. I didn't have time for gentle. I grabbed the rough wood and managed to climb up, scrambling over the still-unconscious Senna.

The driver couldn't possibly see us. But I had to be worried about fairies. Particularly the black-tunics. If they noticed me it was all over.

"Can't control that," I told myself.

I stacked Senna on a pile of rugs. And I began to worm my way down between her rug and the others.

It was hot very quickly. Airless. Miserable. But no one stopped us. And I hadn't noticed outgoing wagons being searched at the thorny gate.

Half an hour later I felt Senna stir.

"Make a sound and we'll both end up in dungeons or worse," I whispered.

She remained silent. Silent for sweltering hours till we were safely beyond the boundaries of Fairy Land.

Finally I crawled out of the pile. Looked back. Yes, we were clear of Fairy Land. There was another wagon maybe two hundred yards back. I doubted the driver of that wagon would concern himself with us.

I hauled Senna down and unwrapped her.

She was bathed in sweat, hair matted down, clothing clinging to her body. Her face was pale, except for the shockingly dark bruise below her chin.

"Sorry," I said. "I don't like to hit anyone. Never a woman. I'm sorry."

Cool, in-control Senna was gone. The gray eyes were narrow. The full lips drawn back, baring her teeth like a snarling wolf. "Sorry?" she hissed. "No. No, you're pleased with yourself, David. You're not sorry. But you will be."

She was wobbly. So was I. But she climbed down off the wagon by herself. She tripped and fell in the dirt. I jumped down beside her and started to help her up. Reached for her. She took my hand. I yanked it back.

Couldn't let her make contact. I backed away. She followed, off the road, into a stand of shade trees.

She was shaking with rage. Her face was muddy. Road dust and sweat.

"You betray me?" she demanded, voice weird. Madness. Insanity. The face of a murderer in the moment before she strikes.

"It's not a betrayal of you. But I'm not betraying April, either."

She erupted in a stream of obscenity, spitting

the words at me, eyes bulging, face red, raging, hurling the filthiest insults imaginable.

I turned and walked away. Nothing I hadn't heard before, I knew all the words, but the shrieking, out-of-control rage was like nothing I'd ever seen.

"Get back here!" she roared.

"I don't think so, Senna."

I kept walking. But now the trees were no longer dappled with late-morning sunlight. Darkness, like a storm cloud. I hesitated. Dark. Almost like night.

And the trees . . . through the trees, a cabin made of logs.

My stomach lurched. A cabin? That cabin? Here? No, impossible. But there was the flag hanging limp beside the front door. There was the number of the cabin. The name of the camp.

No, no, no. Impossible. What . . . what . . .

I tried to stop myself, but now I couldn't, now my legs were moving all on their own, faster, almost running, yes, I was running. Running on rubber legs to the cabin. Everyone asleep. Everyone asleep but that one stupid kid in his bunk.

I was at the door. Just suddenly there. Open. Staring through the door, seeing his back, the back of the counselor in the white windbreaker.

He was tiptoeing. Moving silently through

rows of snoring, wheezing, sleeping kids. Toward the one, the one kid who was awake. He was trying to be asleep, he really was.

"No," I said. "Leave him alone."

But he was going for the kid. The little kid. The little weakling, the little wimp, the little wussy who wouldn't fight, wouldn't stand up for himself.

I had to do something. I had to stop Donny, had to yell, had to grab a stick, had to pick up something heavy and slam it down on his goddamned head, had to kill him, had to stop it stop it stop it.

*Get up, you weakling, get up, you wimp, you disgusting coward, get up and fight, I can't help you, can't help you, all I can do is watch, that's all, all I can do is wait and watch and cry and cry, sniveling coward.*

I could shout, "Leave him alone!" I could do that, couldn't I? Why couldn't I? Why couldn't I?

"Because you're weak, David," a voice whispered. Senna's voice. "That's why he picked you, because you're weak."

"Him, he was weak. Him, the kid, the kid was weak, that's why. He couldn't even —"

The voice laughed. "Are you that blind? Are you that deluded? Look at his face, David."

*No, no, no.*

"See the crying little boy? See him cower? Do you see his face, David? Who is that, David? Who is that you see? Who is the sniveling little weakling?"

"Aaaahhhh!"

I jumped up out of the cot, screaming, screaming, "Stop, stop, stop!" I beat at him, beat at him with my fists, hammered him, ripped at him, and hit nothing but air.

The cabin was gone.

I was standing beneath trees dappled with late-morning sunlight. My fists were bruised, torn from slamming the tree trunk.

Silence. Only the soft rustling of leaves.

I was alone. Senna was nowhere to be seen. But of course she could be anywhere. She could be one of the trees. She had that power, that I knew. The power to confuse men's minds and appear to be anything.

That power and, I knew now, the power to see my dreams. And through those dreams, the truth.

I felt dead. My heart . . . I was dead, wasn't I? Dead and going through the motions of life. Playing the hero and nobody giving a damn.

# Chapter XXI

It's funny, you know. We're free. We make choices. We weigh things in our minds, consider everything carefully, use all the tools of logic and education. And in the end, what we mostly do is what we have no choice but to do.

Makes you think, *Why bother?* But you bother because you do, that's why. Because you're a DNA-brand computer running Childhood 1.0 software. They update the software but the changes are always just around the edges.

You have the brain you have, the intelligence, the talents, the strengths and weaknesses you have, from the moment they take you out of the box and throw away the Styrofoam padding.

But you have the fears you picked up along the way. The terrors of age four or six or eight are never superseded, just layered over. The dread I'd felt so recently, a dread that should be so much greater because the facts had been so much more horrible, still could not diminish the impact of memories that had been laid down long years before.

It's that way all through life, I guess. I have a relative who says she still gets depressed every September because in the back of her mind it's time for school to start again. She's my great-aunt. The woman is sixty-seven and still bumming over the first day of school five-plus decades ago.

It's sad in a way because the pleasures of life get old and dated fast. The teenage me doesn't get the jolt the six-year-old me got from a package of Pop Rocks. The me I've become doesn't rush at the memories of the day I skated down a parking ramp however many years ago.

Pleasure fades, gets old, gets thrown out with last year's fad. Fear, guilt, all that stuff stays fresh.

Maybe that's why people get so enraged when someone does something to a kid. Hurt a kid and he hurts forever. Maybe an adult can shake it off. Maybe. But with a kid, you hurt them and it turns them, shapes them, becomes part of the deep, underlying software of their lives. No delete.

I don't know. I don't know much. I feel like I

know less all the time. Rate I'm going, by the time I'm twenty-one I won't know a damned thing.

But still I was me. Had no choice, I guess. I don't know, maybe that's bull and I was just feeling sorry for myself. But, bottom line, I dried my eyes, and I pushed my dirty, greasy hair back off my face, and I started off down the road again because whatever I was, whoever I was, however messed up I might be, I wasn't leaving April behind.

Maybe it was all an act programmed into me from the get-go, or maybe it grew up out of some deep-buried fear, I mean maybe at some level I was really just as pathetic as Senna thought I was. Maybe I was a fake. Whatever. Didn't matter.

I was going back to the damned dragon, and then I was getting April out, and everything and everyone else could go screw themselves.

One good thing: For now at least, I was done being scared.

I drove myself hard. Walked as long and as fast as I could. Drank whatever water I could find. Ate fruit off the trees and wild onions. I had time but I didn't want to waste any. Maybe Nidhoggr would come, maybe not. If he didn't kill me outright I wanted a chance to go back to Fairy Land and do whatever I could. Help Jalil. Make some doomed attack on the fairy castle. I didn't know, just knew I wasn't going to give up, however it came out with Large and Crusty.

I had time to think. Walking across meadows, through fields, beneath trees, alone, no one to talk to, you have time to think.

So far all I'd done was cope. React. Deal. I was getting tired of that. I mean, okay, I'd been pretty much up to my rear end in alligators so I couldn't blame myself too much for failing to come up with a ten-point plan.

And I was still deep in reptiles. At least I guessed dragons were some kind of reptile. But maybe it was time, just the same, to start thinking long-term. About the others. About Senna. About what might prove to be a long time in the asylum called Everworld. It was just hard to plan when the next event was going back to see Nidhoggr.

It was night when I reached the place where we'd first met Idalia and run into the satyrs. Which meant I wasn't far from the cave that led down to Nidhoggr's lair. And to Hel's domains beyond that.

Not my favorite tourist destination. And I was beat. Not in a state to go underground. I wanted to see the sun shining bright in the sky before I walked down into that realm. Maybe that was silly. But I wasn't going to walk from night into hell.

I began stripping low-hanging branches of the more tender end-twigs. I piled the twigs and leaves all together. Wasn't exactly clean sheets on a Beautyrest, but leaves are better than hard, cold ground. They'd insulate me a little and keep the dampness from wicking up through my clothes.

That was fine. But there was no way to sleep and keep a watch at the same time. I'd have to take my chances. Maybe I could start a fire, which might scare off a wild animal but would just draw a satyr or whatever closer.

I fell asleep and endured half a day of school. At lunch I talked to April. She was fine, she said, the other April. She was fine but scared and lonely and violently pissed. I told her we were on it, me and Jalil and Christopher. Maybe that would help, knowing that.

When I awoke again in Everworld I was shivering, shuddering. Teeth chattering. Cold? It wasn't that cold, was it?

The shakes grabbed me and squeezed me. My teeth chattered uncontrollably. Chills. Fever, that's what it was. I had a fever.

And the nearest aspirin was a universe away. No, wait, April still had Advil. All I had to do was ask her. She . . . April? Do you have that Advil? But no, of course not, April was . . . somewhere.

I was sick. Bad sick. Too sick to think straight.

I felt my insides rumble. I got to my hands and knees and crawled away from my bed. Couldn't do that here, I knew that much. Crawled away, fumbled with my belt . . .

Awake in the park. Little kids playing on the elaborate jungle gym. I was walking in bright sunlight. No, I was running, shirt off, hot day, throwing the baseball.

My own stink. Lying in it. Dark. The chills had subsided. Now I could just feel the burning. So hot I wanted to take my clothes off but that was a bad idea. I felt for the sword. Yes, still had it.

Back across. Wide-awake, healthy, normal. In the real world. Real-world David understood what was happening. Everworld David was sick, delirious, passing into and out of sleep, back and forth across the barrier between universes.

I was worried. About him. Me. The David who was crapping and puking his insides out. Anyone could show up, anyone could do anything they wanted to me. I was helpless. Defenseless. As weak as a baby.

Hooked up with Jalil. He'd had no updates. Everworld Jalil was working around the clock. I told him to tell himself that the other me was sick. Not to count on me.

Dark trees. A face looking down at me. Senna? Senna with those huge gray eyes filled with concern? No. Hallucination. Dream. Wish. All of the above.

Real-world me was frazzled. This was crazy! CNN — Breaking News every half hour. This had been going on for two days now. How much time had elapsed in Everworld? How long had I been lying there, sick, dammit, I had to get up and get on with it. Ticktock. My heart, no the ruby in my chest, would turn to dragon's fire, burn me alive from the inside out.

And what would that do to me, to real-world David? It might kill us both. No way to know. Or it might mean escape from Everworld. Escape from the mad world of gods and myths and aliens. Imprisonment forever in the real world. How would I live now? How would I go through the motions, the school, the tests, the college, the jobs, the life, the already-tired life that awaited me?

Everworld. Dry heaves. Nothing to puke. Nothing left inside me. Rain pouring down, making mud everywhere. I lay on my back, mouth open, trying to slake burning thirst with a drop a drop another drop. Hour after hour. Rain on my face, my chest, all around me, running into my eyes and ears. Drop . . . drop in my dust-caked mouth.

Real world. My dad was in town for a visit. We were sailing in a boat some navy friend of his owned. Out on Lake Michigan, bearing away south to bring the skyline of Chicago into fuller view. The horns of the Hancock, the building blocks of the Sears Tower.

Going through the motions of conversation with my dad, digesting the latest update from Everworld, fearing the next. Sweating when it wasn't hot, a sympathetic reaction, feeling my own pain.

Ticktock. *I know you're sick, dammit, but get up. Get up! Move or it may all be over.*

Jalil, it was all going to come down to him. He would save us, save us from Nidhoggr's fire, maybe. Maybe. But not April, we knew that in our hearts. We could use Jalil's telegraph to ransom Nidhoggr's toys, but April? She would go to Ka Anor.

I looked at my dad. He was still navy, despite being long retired. He was still navy.

You don't leave your own behind.

As the leprechaun said, Dad, "Bull manure."

I was up, up and crawling, with the sun beating down on me through a gap in the branches overhead. Was I awake? Yes, now, but I'd started moving while still asleep.

The rain had stopped. Now the sun was baking the mud and I was crawling. Where were my clothes? I was down to the gym shorts I'd been wearing when we crossed over that first time. Did I take them off in my fever? Shoes. One shoe. No, there was the other, right there in my hand.

I saw mental images of satyrs laughing. Pictures of Senna, concerned. Flashes of April holding Advil in her palm. All of it false, of course. Or maybe most of it.

I crawled. Beneath the shade of trees. The sword. I found it. I buckled it on with numb fingers. It may have taken me half an hour and God, the weight of it dragged at me.

I crawled and stopped. Crawled and stopped. So thirsty. And hungry now, too. Starving. A good sign, right?

Chicken soup. What a cliché. Mom's chicken soup came from a can. Chop a can open with my sword.

The sun was gone. Shade. Sleep.

And when I awoke again in Everworld I was aware. I was me. One of me, anyway.

I stood up, shaky, trembling, almost falling down again. I leaned on the wall of the cave.

"Hope it's the right cave," I croaked.

I staggered, stumbled, fell so many times I stopped caring whether my knees were being shredded. I was cold again. The fever was gone and the cave was cool and I was barely dressed.

At least twice I fell asleep. The real-world me was getting pretty exasperated. He/I was scared. He/I was feeling powerless to affect things. He/I felt sorry for me. He/I was distracted from real life by the latest sudden onslaught of breaking news: This just in, another weird hallucination followed by two more hours of hurting myself.

And on top of it all, meetings with a desperate April. With Christopher who said, "No, man, it's not going well anymore. There's trouble."

And all the while, as I progressed, as I made my way into the Underworld, it was not Nidhoggr's face that loomed up before me like a waking nightmare. It was Hel. Nidhoggr could only kill me. Hel could do so much worse.

Despite everything I was growing stronger. The hunger was awesome. The thirst I slaked a bit by licking condensation from the walls of the cave. I remembered Senna's reminder about Persephone. How she was kidnapped, taken to the Underworld, and because she ate the food there was doomed to return for part of each year.

Great story. Maybe true. I didn't care. I'd have drunk water from Hel's own hand.

Down and down. Down I went, closer to her. Closer to the dragon. Forever. I would never make it. Jalil would pull it off, all unnecessary.

And yet, where was Jalil? Where was Christopher? They should have arrived, bearing the Daghdha's magic talismans. But the cave was empty. What had Christopher said the last time I'd seen him on the other side? Something . . . my brain was a mess. Like someone had thrown a wild, drunken party in there.

"You're walking down the wrong damn cave, that's why there's no one here," I muttered.

And then, I turned a corner. A corner into a

room filled with more gold than Fort Knox had ever seen, and all the jewels in the world.

"Nidhoggr," I whispered.

No answer.

I began to climb the mountain of gold. And then he noticed me. The vast head rose high, high above me. A stray five gallons of dragon's napalm dribbled between his teeth and melted its way into the gold.

"Human," the dragon said. "I do not see my stone, my spear, my sword, or my cauldron."

"No," I said, speaking as loudly as I could.

"You are not looking well."

"No."

"You have mere hours left, human. The stone in your chest is impatient to burn you."

I nodded. "Yeah. I know all that. I also know how you can get your stuff back."

The dragon looked at me. "Have you come to urge me to fall into the trap the fairies have laid for me?"

"No. I know about the trap. They're in bed with the Hetwan. That's partly what this is all about."

The huge eye before me widened in surprise.

"The fairies want your treasure. The Hetwan want to invade the Underworld, and they don't want to have to fight you to do it."

Nidhoggr nodded very slightly, like seeing the Goodyear blimp bob up and down. "The Hetwan. Ka Anor. He has designs on Hel."

"That's the plan. I think the Hetwan helped the fairies construct a weapon to kill you if you showed up over in Fairy Land."

"Tell me about this weapon," Nidhoggr rumbled.

"No. Not until we make a deal."

"The deal is I let you live!" the dragon roared in a voice that knocked me flat on my back.

I was a while in getting back up. "The deal is you bust my friend out of the dungeons of the fairy king and queen."

Nidhoggr frowned. "The redhead or the witch?"

"The redhead."

He nodded his bouncing blimp head again. "Good choice. Witches are never anything but trouble. Their hearts are hard. I'd have had to use a diamond to exchange for that one's heart."

I almost laughed. Nidhoggr had spared Senna through cheapness.

"You get April, I mean the redhead, out. Me and my friends get our hearts. I tell you how to scare the living crap out of the fairies and get your stuff back. With no risk to you."

The dragon thought that over for a while. "I give you my word. May my scales fall off."

"Yeah, that's cool. But first you have to swear an oath you won't break. Swear by your treasure. May you lose your entire treasure."

"Ah. Yes. I swear by my treasure."

I swayed, still unsteady. I caught myself before plunging off the edge of the mound. "They have huge arrows, disguised as towers. Topped with diamond-tipped arrowheads. Chances are you'd never have noticed them. They're right in the middle of the palace."

"If I cannot fly over the palace, how am I to regain my treasures?"

"Forget the palace. The palace, the whole city, that's all nothing. That's not what the fairies are afraid of losing. They're businessmen, my large friend."

# Chapter XXIII

The dragon decided I was telling the truth. I don't know, maybe he had some way of knowing whether I was lying, just like he knew that Senna was a witch. Or maybe it's what we've all noticed: Cynicism is a weak force in Everworld. It was one of our very few advantages.

The big dragon instructed me to climb up on his head. I told him I needed food. Two of the conveniently appearing troll butlers showed up with a loaf of bread and a piece of cheese.

Then the monsters carried me up the steep, diamond-encrusted slope of Nidhoggr's jaw. Nidhoggr was in a hurry now. The fairies had made a fool of him and the dragon hadn't gotten as big and as rich as he was by letting himself get jerked around by every clever munchkin that came along.

A point he was anxious to make.

I settled in behind the windscreen formed by his left brow, a curved wall of scaled flesh that was visible only in the spaces between diamonds and emeralds and rubies.

The dragon unfolded wings that could easily have been the playing fields for several simultaneous football games. The wings at least were not entirely covered in jewels. They were pterodactyl-looking things, flesh stretched between ribbing, primitive. And, as big as they were, far too small to lift this behemoth. At least in the universe where I'd grown up.

Nidhoggr shoved his snout up against the cave opening, the one I'd just come through, and blew out. A volcanic eruption of magma flooded the cave. I cowered, trying to shield myself from the heat. But still I smelled my own singed hair.

"That will protect my treasure while I am away," Nidhoggr said.

And then, with wings at once so vast and tiny, he began to fly. Straight up. A blue whale flying directly vertical with only the leisurely flapping of wings that might, might on a good day have lifted my Buick.

Up and up, not fast but fast enough considering that everything about this flight was impossible. Up and up the long shaft, up into morning light. We rose from the cone of a tumbled, half-eroded volcano.

Up into the sky, and now Nidhoggr was whipping his barbed tail back and forth like he was some monstrous tadpole. Giant wings, giant tail, all propelling the fabulous diamond-glittery monster through the air.

I couldn't see directly down because of the slope of Nidhoggr's head. I couldn't see the effect this apparition was having on the creatures who felt the sudden chill of his passing shadow. But I could imagine. Human, elf, dwarf, satyr, nymph, fairy, or alien, I was pretty sure no one was looking up and feeling secure. I don't think Loki or Hel or Huitzilopoctli could have been indifferent.

I was perched atop a 747 flying at treetop level and dribbling fire.

I ate some bread. I ate some cheese. I felt better. I felt strength returning. Was it something magical in the bread, or just the simple fact of having calories to fuel the machine?

In an hour we were over the border of Fairy Land. The leprechaun with the bad attitude was not going to be collecting an entrance tax on us.

"Remember, stay well away from the palace. Hover over the marketplace. That's their Achilles' heel. That's what they can't risk."

The dragon executed a lazy course correction. I climbed gingerly over the brow and perched dangerously just above the fold of his eyelid.

Now I could see almost directly down, at least to the side. When the dragon lowered his snout I held onto diamond protrusions and could clearly see the marketplace.

Business was at a standstill. Men, dwarfs, elves, fairies, all were running. First this way, then that. Back and forth. Pointless panic. The dragon was circling, circling, not twenty feet above the taller buildings. The wind from his passage ripped the awnings from stalls, sent trade goods whipping up and down the avenues, tripped the panicked vendors.

"Summon the king and queen," Nidhoggr bellowed.

"And my friends," I said in a barely audible squeak.

"And bring the redhead from the dungeons," Nidhoggr added.

There was a blur as fairies raced for the city. Unnecessary, of course, because the people in the city's towers must surely have seen the dragon. And his voice would have been heard anywhere within a hundred square miles.

"You see the towers over there?" I yelled, half deafened.

"I see them," Nidhoggr agreed. "They meant to slay great Nidhoggr. You have kept your bargain and spoken the truth. Nidhoggr will keep his own end of the agreement."

We cruised, always safely far from the palace. Nidhoggr passed the time by incinerating several large flocks of sheep.

When we saw fast-moving carriages racing from the city, the dragon settled down in the center of the market, crushing several buildings and flattening dozens of stalls in the process.

The carriage, drawn by eight of the weird eight-legged horses and escorted by perhaps a hundred fairy warriors, all heavily armored and carrying bows and swords, came to a halt a few hundred feet from the tip of Nidhoggr's nose.

It was a pointless display. Nidhoggr could sneeze and turn the entire detachment of warriors into briquettes.

The king climbed down out of the carriage. Nervous. Behind him, the Hetwan.

My blood ran cold. Had the Hetwan already taken April?

"Great Nidhoggr, you honor us with your presence," the king said, all phony charm and politician's sincerity.

Nidhoggr spoke. "The stone. The spear. The sword. The cauldron."

The king looked theatrically puzzled. "I'm afraid I don't understand."

Nidhoggr turned his head slightly and breathed. Only a shallow, slight exhalation.

Magma poured from his mouth, red-and-black fire, steaming, distorting the air itself.

The magma poured forth, ran along a side street. Buildings on both sides burst into flames. The napalm ate the buildings from the bottom, disintegrated them. The dragon turned his face to the king again.

"I will burn this market. I will burn you. And I will . . . decline . . . to fly above the palace so that you can murder me, king of the fairies."

The Hetwan didn't blink. The fairy king did.

"We have, um . . . we have recently learned that certain items were stolen from you, great Nidhoggr. We knew nothing of this crime but have recently arrested those responsible. Thieves are everywhere in these times."

"Yes. In many fine palaces," the dragon said dryly.

The king waved frantically over his shoulder. A wagon lurched forward. Fairies whipped back a canvas cover revealing a stone, not much to look at, maybe the size of a beer keg, also a spear, a sword, and a battered-looking old pot filled to the rim with reddish-brown stew of some sort.

"Here are your possessions," the king said.

"Thank you, great king."

"My friends!" I yelled.

The king seemed to notice me for the first time.

"I want my friends. April. Christopher. Jalil. I want them."

The king's eyes flickered from me down to the dragon, back to me. "You may assuredly have the two males. However, the female witch, well, the Hetwan have already bargained for her and a price has been agreed upon. A very fair price, if I may say, and since the terms have been agreed on . . ." He shrugged.

I started to say something, but Nidhoggr knew the deal. Whatever else you could say about the old monster, he's a dragon who keeps his word.

"Did the Hetwan pay you the value of this great market?" the dragon rumbled.

"I . . . I'm afraid I don't understand."

At that the queen bustled down from the carriage. She stomped up to the king, looked up at the dragon, her face a mixture of rage and I-told-you-so smugness.

"Give the girl to the dragon, you jackass, or he'll burn you. And what is far worse, he'll burn the market."

"No," the Hetwan said, stepping forward defiantly.

The queen grabbed the king's arm and pulled him back. With a jerk of her head she motioned the guards to retreat. The Hetwan stood alone.

"The witch belongs to my lord, Ka Anor," the Hetwan said.

Nidhoggr laughed. And then he released what may have been a hundred gallons of his napalm. The fire sloshed across the ground and engulfed the Hetwan's legs.

Hetwan do not cry out in pain, I guess. But the sizzling, cracking, bursting sounds as the Hetwan was slowly drawn down into the fire, melting, melting like the witch in *The Wizard of Oz*, was horrible enough.

The alien's three reaching mandibles searched all the while for food. All the way down, till all that was left was the alien's head.

"You really should learn to identify witches properly," Nidhoggr said. "Only a fool buys a witch who is no witch."

The Hetwan's eyes popped, just like kernels of corn. And seconds later the alien's head blew apart from the steam trapped within it.

We were given safe passage to the far boundary of Fairy Land. There the gate was formed of massive trees, not rosebushes. But a very similar leprechaun sat on a stool, smoking a pipe and looking picturesque.

He wished us top o' the mornin'.

Five of us had entered Fairy Land from the other direction. Four of us were leaving. I'd said I wouldn't leave anyone behind. I'd left Senna. But Senna was never really a part of us. A part of me, yes. Maybe always would be. And I would still try to find her, try to save her from her truest enemy: herself.

"So, the telegraph didn't work?" I asked Jalil as we trudged through the gate.

"Oh, it worked. Ambrigar is going to be a very rich fairy. He paid us fair and square. And we'd reached a deal to buy Nidhoggr's stuff back. It was all a done deal. Only they wouldn't give up April. Not for anything."

"Why didn't you get the stuff to Nidhoggr?" I demanded.

Jalil shrugged. "Look, we could save our own lives but April would be lost. Once the Hetwan had her, that was going to be it. And it occurred to us, well, to Christopher actually, that your plan B wasn't going to work if Nidhoggr already had his stuff back."

"Nothing to trade, man," Christopher confirmed. "The Nid just wanted his stuff back. If plan B was going to work he had to still want it."

It took me a couple of minutes to digest all that. It made sense, I guessed.

"They risked it all to save me," April said. "You all did. How am I going to go on thinking that the three of you are idiots when you go and do something like that?"

We laughed. First laugh in a while.

Christopher said, "Well, it wasn't such a big risk. We had faith in the general here. We knew he'd come through."

"Uh-huh."

"Yep. For the first few hours after we decided to put it all on David to win, Jalil and I were pretty confident. Then we find out on the other side that he's sick and delirious and retching his guts out. So then, not so confident. And by late last night with me tossing and turning and waiting for my freaking heart to go nuclear I do seem to recall that some harsh words were spoken."

Jalil nodded. "Yeah, I seem to recall the phrase 'pathetic wanna-be hero who's probably lying around being sick and is off doing the nasty with the witchy woman not giving a damn whether we fry from the inside out.' That was while we were still feeling hopeful. Later things turned nasty."

"So, what did happen to Senna?" April asked me.

"I don't know."

I don't think she believed that. I don't think any of them did. But my stock was pretty high right then. I was everyone's hero. Till the next time I screwed up. Or until Senna came back into my life.

"So you wired up the fairies, and we have nothing to show for it," I said. "Well, that about figures. Still, we're alive. My heart's going bumpity-bump again. Maybe as long as we survive we just shut up and be happy."

There was a silence. A long silence. An expectant silence.

I looked at Christopher, at Jalil. They were both grinning.

"What?"

Jalil matched April's pace and reached into her backpack. He withdrew a hand filled with diamonds. Not exactly impressive when placed against memories of Nidhoggr's mountain. But better than the spare change and rumpled dollar bills we had.

"Damn."

"Yeah. We're rich. Just one problem. The market is back that way. And I don't think we're welcome there. I don't think they like the company we keep: witches and big dragons and all."

We walked on into the night. We left Fairy Land behind. And as night fell the landscape changed. But it was dark by the time we stopped for sleep.

Too dark to notice that the trees, the grasses, the flowers all around us were not, never had been, part of any human experience.

We experienced an actual moment or two of peace. Peace is hard to come by in Everworld. Maybe in any world.

I looked up to see the moon. Our moon? Some reasonable facsimile? Or an illusion created out of magic?

It was a moon. That was enough. It was white. It shined down on us. And it gave me peace.

Until I saw the shadows crossing its luminous face.

Jailil was not far away, looking up, like me.

"Jalil, do you . . ." I whispered.

"Yeah. I see them," he said. "I see them."

Two disciplined columns of dark figures that might almost have been huge bats. Might, in a different universe. But these were creatures with shiny compound eyes and gossamer wings and ever-questing insect mouths. These were the cold, deadly servants of the god-eater.

Above us, behind and before, the Hetwan legions flew. We had walked blithely toward a danger that made even terrifying immortals cringe and quake.

We had entered the land of Ka Anor.

# #VI

# Fear the Fantastic

The far horizon was phasing from gray to pink. Any minute now the sun would peek up over the rim of the world. Or maybe it was some god dragging a big light across the sky, who knew? Maybe the world was still round, here, and the sun was still the sun. Or maybe not.

"I would sell my mother for a glass of milk," I muttered. "Two percent, whole milk, even one percent. Anything but skim as long as it is ice cold. Bye mom, but I need my milk. I'm a growing boy."

The sun edged up. And then a howling, a keening, a wailing.

I jumped to my feet. David jerked up. April spun, stumbled to her feet and brushed the tumbled haystack of auburn hair out of her face. Jalil sat up.

"What is that?" David asked me.

I shook my head. The sound was growing, swelling, seeming to roll across the face of the earth, a far off choir that was galloping toward us.

All on our feet. All very, very awake. David took his sword back.

The sound was still swelling, not so much from volume as from new "voices" being added. Like a hundred people were singing at one level, and another fifty joined in, and another fifty, and more and more.

And as it grew, the sound changed subtly. You didn't so much think "moaning" as "singing." Like a psalm in church: a little mournful, a little shaky, but gaining confidence as it approached some well-remembered chorus.

The sun, golden fire, suddenly burned on the horizon, and the sound, the voices, the choir, whatever it was let out a gasp of joy.

"Ah!" April cried, almost joining in unconsciously.

Pink and pale blue and orange streaked the gray sky and the sound, the sound was becoming emotional. It wasn't threatening, it wasn't dangerous-sounding, but it was huge and everywhere without being loud. I was a bug walking across a woofer and fearing that someone was going to crank the volume up to ten. It was all around me, everywhere the sun's rays reached, everywhere that the shadows gave way was filled with The Sound.

And now I could see well enough to become very, very nervous. We were in the middle of a landscape that looked like what you'd get if Salvador Dalí and Dr. Seuss had worked together.

It was flat, basically. Flat as Kansas. Except that someone had come along with a gigantic ice cream scoop and hollowed out deep, plunging, almost perfectly round valleys. Then the ice cream had been piled up here and there in improbable, rounded hills one, two, three scoops high.

We were within twenty feet of the edge of one of the big holes. We hadn't even known it. The bush where I'd gone to do my business in the night was maybe one body length away from a sheer drop.

But as weird as this basic geography was, it was what covered the hills and the land and filled the valleys that made it clear we were a very, very long way from Old Orchard Mall.

They were trees. Like palm trees in that they had long, serpentine trunks. Like maples or elms or oaks in that at the top they suddenly sprouted robust branches. The leaves ranged from pointy, French cooking knife shapes, to fans, to six-pointed stars, to large, flat pie plates with cutouts in the shape of triangles or eye slits.

The leaves were sea foam green and pink and burnt orange and rain slicker yellow. And some were mirrors that caught the sun's strengthening rays and seemed almost to catch fire, so that as I looked down into the neatly circular valley, or back at the triple-scoop mountain, or at the trees swaying over my head, I was dazzled and blinded by glittering, reflected light.

It was the trees that were making The Sound. As the light neared they moaned in anticipation. As they lit up, they cried out in wordless joy. Then, as the sun blazed off their mirrors, and through their cutouts, the trees mellowed into a satisfied hum.

And all of this seemed to extend forever before us and around us. The only zone of silence and relative calm was back in the direction from which we'd come.

"It's beautiful," April said, her tone neatly balanced between delight and incredulity.

"This is Hetwan country?" I wondered.

"Guess so," David said. "Not exactly what I was expecting."

"What were you expecting?" Jalil asked him.

"I don't know. Like a termite mound or an ant colony. I mean, they're insects. Aren't they?"

"They're aliens," Jalil answered. "I'm not sure if they're insects, really. They look like our concept of bugs. Aside from the fact that they walk erect."

"Really big bugs."

"It's beautiful," Jalil said. "It's amazing. Doesn't mean the creatures that live here are friendly."

"Yeah."

"The jungle's pretty, too. Spiders, leopards, snakes."

I said, "You know, after the old Midgard Serpent it's gonna take an awful lot of snake to impress me."

"So what do we do? Where do we go?" April asked. She yawned.

"The devil we know versus the devil we don't," David said. "Go back and the fairies for sure get us. Go forward, we don't know."

"The fairy queen said Ka Anor only eats gods," April pointed out.

"Hey, yeah!" I said. "That's right. She was a sharp old crone. She must know, right? Anyway, the Hetwan who was there didn't say anything different."

"The Hetwan aren't talkative," Jalil said. "But I think you guys are probably right. I think the fairy queen knew what she was talking about. The fairies weren't acting like the Hetwan were nothing, but they weren't falling to their knees every time Ka Anor's name came up."

We were talking ourselves into walking deeper into Hetwan country. It was the singing and the landscape. It was affecting us, lulling us, dulling the Gillette edge of my usual fear. I knew all this.

But it really was hard to see anything terrible happening in a place where the trees sing.

"Ka Anor is the root of the whole problem," April said. "Ka Anor has destabilized things. He is the Everworld revolution. If he was gone . . ."

This snapped me out of my dreamy "isn't it all just ever so lovely?" state of mind.

"Don't even start down that road again, April," I warned. "Our mission, should we decide to accept it — and of course we don't have a choice — is to stay alive and haul our pansy asses back to the land of seat belts, multi-vitamins, and looking both ways before you cross the street. I'm thinking that us all going off to kill some schizo-alien-god-eater who's surrounded by an army of thousands of flying bug-monkeys is not the best way to retain the aforementioned pansy ass."

Jalil cocked an eyebrow. "I didn't know you knew the word 'aforementioned.' Let alone that you could use it in a sentence."

"Even crackers take business English," I shot back. "What, so you're okay with this, Jalil? Us going off to solve all the problems of Everworld armed with a sword and your two inch knife?"

He shook his head. "No. I'm not okay with it."

"Me neither," David admitted. "Basic military common sense: four people do not decide to attack a force of tens of thousands. I'm thinking we keep moving, keep our heads down, try to find the shortest way out of all this, back into whatever piece of earth may be nearby. What's that noise?'"

"The trees," April said. "Weird. They're sharp."

"Say what?"

Suddenly the volume of the trees rose and sure enough, they were sharp. They were building up to out-and-out screeching, screaming, howling. But all from one direction. Like a wave of sonic misery rolling toward us.

I saw treetops in the distance. Then, very suddenly, I saw the wood chippers. . . .

Army ants. That was the first impression. Only these were way too big to be ants. These things were the size of ponies. And roughly a third of that size was devoted to a mouth about as big around as a manhole cover.

There were hundreds. Maybe thousands. A herd. A swarm. A wave, crashing through and swirling around the trees. Climbing over each on their uncounted rat feet.

Three of them annihilated one of the mirror pink trees in thirty seconds. Chewed it up like beavers on crack. One chopped it down with a series of lightning-fast chomps, then, even as the tree fell, another would leap up and start gnawing on its midsection. The third would catch the tree top, the branches, and launch into the leaves.

I flashed for one hideous, frozen instant on the woodchipper scene from *Fargo*.

Then I ran.

I was not alone. The four of us tore back the way we'd come, back toward Fairy Land, each having the identical thought that if we had to die, a fairy arrow through the neck was a lot better than being chewed up and crapped out as sawdust.

The trees were screaming all around us now, how did trees scream, did they have mouths, too? Run! Don't ask dumb questions, run! Howling and shrieking all around us, the trees, they knew the monsters were coming this way, knew they were about to be pulped. Them and anything that got in the way.

"The pit!" David yelled.

The pits? He thought this was the pits? That was his comment? The pits? What was he, Richie Cunningham all of a sudden?

Oh, the pit! The hole, the valley. Yeah, yeah, run!

The edge of the drop was on my left. Just past April who wasn't wasting any more time than I was. Two things are really scary: running away, and seeing someone else run away. You see someone else, their face all distorted by fear, eyes wide, cheeks red, mouth pulled back in a toothy, skeletal grin, well, that's not reassuring.

I heard David cry out. I shot a look toward the sound. I saw him go down like a skier who can't quite outrun the avalanche. He just toppled backward, arms flung out, mouth open, fell back and was gone.

Then they were on us, a wall of teeth and sweaty fur and frenzied energy. They were a rolling lava spill of destruction, ripping, chewing, straining to find the next thing to destroy, and the next thing was me.

Twenty feet. So fast! Ten.

I cut left. Slammed into April. She said a word she saves for serious situations. We sprawled. I bounced up like a drop of water in a hot frying pan. Down–Up. A single movement, fall and rise. Like I was made of rubber.

Not fast enough, I could feel hot breath on me, teeth filling my field of vision. I screamed a girly scream and leaped.

Into nothingness.

April and I fell, screaming. About ten feet. Maybe more, maybe less, I wasn't reeling out the tape measure. I was screaming like the entire cast of *I Know What You Did Three Summers Ago.*

I hit. Heels first. Face into bushes. Rolled. Branches, leaves, dirt, dirt jamming into my mouth, fingers clawing, legs kicking, looking for a level surface.

Down and down. Stop. I was against a tree trunk. Looking . . . down? Up? My eyes had stopped working for me, they were on their own, refusing to focus. Then, they snapped. Focus.

Focus on a wall of the wood chippers spilling

off the cliff above me like lemmings. The tree I was leaning against, my back possibly broken, and my kidneys definitely bruised, started yowling. I could feel the tree's voice vibrating my spine.

I did Scooby Doo legs, feet flying. My heel caught something, I spun, on my side, on the dirt, spun, legs over head, rolled and tumbled away from the tree that three seconds later was falling and being chomped in mid-air.

I tried to stand. The wave hit me. Giant beavers stuck on "fast forward" nailed me to the ground. I rolled onto my belly and they were all over me. . . .